"This is all too weird. I need time. I've changed my mind, I think…"

"Not an option."

Without any warning he bent his head and pressed his mouth to hers.

The hot, hungry kiss did not start slowly and build. It was hard and demanding, and began at a mind-blowing level of intimacy that nothing could have prepared her for. As his mouth moved with innate sensuality across her own, heat flared inside her, and her senses were flooded with the texture and taste of him.

All about the author...
Kim Lawrence

KIM LAWRENCE comes from English/Irish stock. Though lacking much authentic Welsh blood, she was born and brought up in north Wales. She returned there when she married, and her sons were both born on Anglesey, an island off the coast. Though not isolated, Anglesey is a little off the beaten track, but lively Dublin, which Kim loves, is only a short ferry ride away.

Today they live on the farm her husband was brought up on. Welsh is the first language of many people in this area, and Kim's husband and sons are all bilingual—she is having a lot of fun, not to mention a few headaches, trying to learn the language!

With small children, the unsocial hours of nursing didn't look attractive, so—encouraged by a husband who thinks she can do anything she sets her mind to—Kim tried her hand at writing. Always a keen Harlequin reader, she thought it seemed natural for her to write a romance novel. Now she can't imagine doing anything else.

She is a keen gardener and cook and enjoys running—often on the beach, as on an island the sea is never very far away. She is usually accompanied by her Jack Russell, Sprout—don't ask, it's a long story!

Kim Lawrence

MISTRESS: PREGNANT BY THE SPANISH BILLIONAIRE

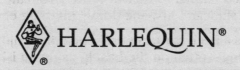

HARLEQUIN®

TORONTO • NEW YORK • LONDON
AMSTERDAM • PARIS • SYDNEY • HAMBURG
STOCKHOLM • ATHENS • TOKYO • MILAN • MADRID
PRAGUE • WARSAW • BUDAPEST • AUCKLAND

Recycling programs
for this product may
not exist in your area.

ISBN-13: 978-0-373-12919-5

MISTRESS: PREGNANT BY THE SPANISH BILLIONAIRE

First North American Publication 2010.

Copyright © 2009 by Kim Lawrence.

www.eHarlequin.com

Printed in U.S.A.

MISTRESS: PREGNANT BY THE SPANISH BILLIONAIRE

CHAPTER ONE

THE doctor was leaving the Castillo d'Oro when the sound of a helicopter low overhead stopped him in his tracks. As he paused, his hand shading his eyes from the sun, it landed and a tall figure disembarked.

The figure, immediately recognisable even at a distance, appeared to see him and hit the ground running, reaching the doctor's side before the helicopter had lifted off again. He had covered the hundred metres or so with a speed and grace that in the medic's envious opinion would not have looked out of place on an athletic track.

'How are you, Luiz?'

The question was strictly rhetorical.

There were few people who looked as little in need of his care as Luiz Felipe Santoro. Despite his exertion, the hand extended to the doctor was cool and dry, and its owner, not even breathing hard, presented his usual immaculate appearance complete with formal tailored suit and sober silk tie.

The doctor always found the vitality this young man projected slightly exhausting and today was no exception.

It was hard to guess looking at him now that Luiz Santoro had once been a delicate child who had suffered more than his fair share of childhood ailments including asthma.

His delicate constitution combined with an adventurous—

some called it reckless—personality meant the doctor had treated the young Luiz for many bumps and bruises, and on one occasion a broken limb.

It seemed likely to the doctor that it was that streak of adventure that his parents, before they had left him in the care of his grandmother, had tried unsuccessfully to quash that made Luiz, to quote his grandmother, 'the only member of this family I can stomach.'

That, of course, was on the occasions her favourite grandson hadn't incited her wrath by refusing to jump through one of her hoops, but then when the two people involved were strong-minded individuals, both incapable of compromise, there were bound to be sparks.

It struck the doctor as ironic really that the only member of the family that neither wanted nor needed the fortune the rest of his family eyed so covetously was likely to inherit. Luiz, with his steel-trap mind and competitive streak, had made his first million before he was twenty-one and was already incredibly wealthy in his own right.

'I'm surprised to see you. Your office told me you were mid Atlantic on your way to New York when I rang.'

'I was.' Luiz dismissed his altered travel arrangements with a wave of his long brown fingers. 'How is my grandmother?'

The medic felt the sweat break out across his brow as he met, with as much composure as he could summon, the younger man's dark eyes. It seemed to him that there was more than a hint of the ruthlessness the press spoke of in his dark, penetrating gaze.

The doctor tried hard to put a positive spin on his account of his patient's health, but Doña Elena's health was not what it had been.

Luiz summed up the situation in his usual concise manner. 'So you are saying, though she has improved slightly since you contacted me, it is possible my grandmother might not get better.'

Luiz had always prided himself on being a realist, but this oddly was the first time he had allowed himself to believe that his grandmother was not indestructible. Recognising that should not hit him so hard—her decline was inevitable—but that did not stop him feeling as if he'd just been kicked in the guts.

The doctor sighed and looked sympathetic. 'I'm sorry it could not be better news, Luiz,' he said, struggling to gauge the younger man's reaction. It was not easy when his eyes gave as much away as the mirrored surface of dark sunglasses. 'Of course if I am needed…'

Luiz, his expression sombre, inclined his head in acknowledgement of the courtesy. 'Goodbye, Doctor.'

He was still standing watching the man leave, thinking about the great gaping hole the death of his grandmother would leave, when a cheery voice hailed him.

'Luiz!'

He turned in response to his name to see Ramon, his grandmother's estate manager, approaching at a trot.

Ramon had replaced the previous manager five years earlier. Experiencing a lot of resistance in the early days of his tenure, he had appealed to Luiz for support in his efforts to bring about some much-needed changes to the *estancia* set high in the Sierra Nevada, where tradition was important and his modernising ways were viewed with suspicion.

Over the years the two men had developed not just a relaxed working relationship, but a friendship. When Luiz had discovered the desperate condition of his grandmother's finances—she had taken some appalling advice and put all her financial eggs in one basket; they had smashed—Ramon's expertise and energy had helped him to save the *estancia* from imminent financial ruin.

Luiz was grateful that his grandmother still remained blissfully ignorant of the personal funds he had poured into the failing estate and how close she had come to losing it.

'Surprise visit,' the other man observed as he approached.

'You could say that,' Luiz agreed, unfastening his tie from his throat and loosing the top button of his shirt.

'Your grandmother…?'

Luiz nodded.

Ramon winced and clapped a sympathetic hand to the other man's shoulder before tentatively asking, 'Not a good time, I know, but I was wondering should I go ahead with the preparations for next week's birthday celebrations or…?'

'Go ahead with them,' Luiz agreed before turning the subject to matters he felt more comfortable discussing. 'Has anything else come up?'

'It's funny you should say that.'

Luiz, clasping a hand to the back of his head as he rotated it to relieve the tension that was tying his shoulder muscles in knots, missed the flicker of amusement that crossed Ramon's face. Brow puckered in concentration, he glanced at his wristwatch.

'Give me an hour to see my grandmother, change and shower…'

'This item that has come up is actually of the immediate variety.'

There was a flicker of interest in Luiz's eyes as he asked, 'How immediate?'

'Immediate as in there is a woman, a *pretty* woman, demanding to see you.'

'A woman!'

'Pretty woman.'

'I was thinking more along the lines of a problem with the plumbing or a disaster with the first press of olives,' Luiz admitted. 'And does this woman…sorry, *pretty* woman—and I have to say, Ramon, it pains me that you would think that would make a difference—have a name?'

'She is a Miss Nell Frost. English, I believe.'

Luiz shook his head and shrugged dismissively. The name rang no bells. 'Never heard of her.'

'Pity. I was hoping she was your birthday present for Doña Elena's birthday—the next Mrs Santoro. Now that *would* make her day.' When his joke fell flat Ramon shrugged and asked, 'Got any other ideas?'

'Ideas?' Luiz, who couldn't see the problem, frowned. 'Just tell her it is not convenient, suggest she makes an appointment.'

He began to walk away but Ramon followed him.

'It won't work. Neither will threats, charm or bribery because I've already tried and failed.'

Luiz felt a surge of impatience. How hard could it be to get rid of one unwanted visitor?

'Have Security remove her.' His expression revealed that he was amazed this had not already been done. 'Or better still, get Sabina to give her her marching orders.'

'Sabina has tried. It was she who suggested that you might like to speak with the young lady.'

Luiz raised a brow. Sabina held the official title of housekeeper, but in reality she was far more and in this household her suggestions carried as much weight as his grandmother's orders. He gave a resigned sigh. 'Where is she?'

'She has been sitting on the south lawn for the last hour or so, and it's warm.'

Luiz raised his brows at the understatement. It was thirty-plus degrees in the shade. 'Why has she been sitting on the south lawn?'

'I believe it is in the nature of a protest.'

'A protest,' Luiz echoed. 'Against what?'

The other man struggled against a smile. 'Why, something to do with you, I believe. Did I mention she is very pretty?' he added.

CHAPTER TWO

NELL lifted her hand to shade her eyes from the sun that beat down on her unprotected head. The throbbing pain in her temples and behind her eyes felt uncomfortably similar to the early stages of a migraine.

She dragged her hand down her forehead to blot the salty rivulets that ran down her face. Her skin felt gritty and hot.

How long had she been sitting here? This morning certainly seemed like several lifetimes ago, she thought, pulling the creased and crumpled e-mail printout from her pocket. She had lost track of time; actually she was finding it increasingly difficult to focus her wandering thoughts.

She didn't know who had been more surprised when she had sat down and delivered her ultimatum, her or the man with the warm smile. He had been so nice she felt a bit guilty, but mingled with the guilt had been a weird sense of liberation. After spending most of her adult life being accommodating and putting her plans on hold for other people, now it was her turn to be obstinate and awkward.

'I'm actually quite good at it,' she discovered with a smile.

Luiz, who was approaching the solitary figure sitting in the middle of several acres of carefully manicured lawn, stopped when she spoke.

The voice was low and with an unexpectedly sexy rasp that

was a lot more grown up than she appeared to be. Ramon had misled him when he had said woman—the female sitting there was, he decided, a girl.

A girl with hair that shone honeyed gold in the sun, dressed in a light blue summer dress that revealed slim, shapely calves. She might be shapely all the way up to her delectable lips but the dress was not fitted to her slim shape.

As he continued to observe her as yet unseen a sudden gust of warm air lifted the skirt of her unfitted dress and suggested the shapeliness went at least thigh-high.

Had he not had more important things on his mind… Had she not been too young, and possibly unstable—she was talking to herself, after all—Luiz just might, he conceded, have been interested.

But as none of the above conditions applied he could view her with total objectivity.

'From now on everyone is going to give in to me. I'm a powerful and strong woman. God, I'm not even in my prime yet. Where has the man with the warm smile gone—to call for reinforcements or get Luiz Felipe slimy snake Santoro?' Liking the alliteration she smiled and wondered if she'd had too much sun.

'He went to get Luiz Felipe Santoro.' Accustomed to hearing himself described in slightly more flattering terms—at least to his face—Luiz was curious to discover where this young woman had formed this opinion of his character.

Nell, who had been unaware that she was voicing her thoughts out loud until that moment, focused on the shiny leather shoes a few feet away.

'Who are you?' Luiz asked as his brain struggled to provide a scenario that would put this odd girl here, now.

Nell's gaze stayed at knee level. 'I'm the one asking the questions,' she retorted belligerently. 'Who are you?'

'I'm Luiz Santoro.'

A sigh of relief left her dry lips as Nell got shakily to her feet.

The man who had materialised was tall, dark and handsome, though the generic term hardly seemed appropriate considering the unique individuality of his features.

Her glance lingered on his face. The man had a firm, clean-shaven jaw, high forehead, golden skin stretched across strong cheekbones, and a wide sensually sculpted mouth.

As her eyes connected with his hooded, unblinking and slightly impatient stare Nell experienced an odd little jolt that ran like an electric shock all the way down to her toes.

She blinked to break the connection. His eyes really were extraordinary. Set beneath strongly defined black brows, they were deep-set and very dark, almost black, flecked with silver and framed by the only feature that was not aggressively male—long dark curling lashes that any woman would have coveted.

She started to shake her head, only stopping when it made her world spin unpleasantly. 'You can't be Luiz Felipe Santoro.' She'd said it so often that the name was starting to roll off her tongue as if she were a native.

For a start off he was no student or teenager... Had Lucy said he was or had that been an assumption?

And that was the least of it. Her thought processes moved sluggishly as she looked up at him, her critical stare trained on the face of the man whom her niece intended to marry. Actually there was little to criticise on an aesthetic level at least, his face was about as perfect as faces got if you liked a profile that could have come from an ancient Greek statue.

And the rest of him... Nell swallowed, uncomfortable with her visceral response to the rest of him, which was silly. His body was no better than any number of Olympic swimmers she had watched cleave cleanly through the water of a swimming pool.

Of course, they had not been standing mere feet away from her. Other senses like smell—he really did smell exceptionally good in a warm male, musky sort of way—had not been involved.

'I can't be?' The sinfully sexy Spaniard with the autocratic bearing sounded more curious than put out. 'Why not?'

'You have to be, what…?' Her assessing gaze moved up from his toes to the top of his dark gleaming head. All of it appeared to be hard muscle and bone and aggressively male. Her stomach muscles reacted to all that undiluted masculinity and flipped. 'Thirty?'

'Thirty-two.'

'Thirty-two,' she echoed.

Luiz was wondering why she looked so peculiarly repulsed by the admission when she added, 'That is disgusting.'

An energising burst of anger put strength back into Nell's legs as she took a purposeful step towards the Spaniard. Self-satisfaction was not in her experience an attractive trait, and men this good-looking were generally very self-satisfied.

Of course, her experience was limited.

'You know what I think of men who prey on impressionable young girls?'

'I feel sure you are going to tell me,' he drawled laconically.

His flippant attitude incensed Nell further. 'You think this is some sort of joke? This is a young girl's future we are talking about. Lucy is too young to get married.'

'Who is Lucy?'

The blonde pursed her lips and continued to regard him as though he were some sort of depraved monster. The novelty value of being verbally abused was already wearing thin but the pleasure of staring at her heaving bosom would take a lot longer to pall.

The kick of his libido was irrational, but sexual desire did have a habit of bypassing the logic circuits. Fortunately he never had any problem keeping his own carnal instincts on a short leash.

'Don't play the innocent with me.'

With those eyes and those lips, she reflected, her eyes lingering on the sensual curve, such an effort would be a waste of time. A mouth like that had nothing to do with innocence and everything to do with decadence. It also suggested he would be a pretty good kisser—not that Nell had any desire to put her theory to the test, but she could see how an inexperienced girl like Lucy might be fatally tempted.

'Do you even intend to marry her or was that some line to get her into bed?'

'I do not actually intend to marry anyone.'

A tide of angry colour washed over her already hot fair skin as Nell missed the shadow that passed across his face and just heard the shameless admission.

'And actually I have never had to promise marriage to get anyone into bed.'

Now that she could believe—the man had all the qualifications to be a serial seducer. 'So why does Lucy think she's marrying you?'

'I really couldn't say.'

'Maybe this will refresh your memory,' she said, extending the shaking hand that held the e-mail to him.

When he made no attempt to take it Nell let her hand drop down.

'"Dear Aunt Nell—"' she quoted.

'You are Aunt Nell?' She looked like no aunt he had ever met.

Frowning darkly at the interruption, Nell nodded. 'Yes. "Dear Aunt Nell,"' she continued, not referring to the transcript—she had read the damned thing so many times since yesterday the contents were burned into her memory.

'"I arrived here last week. Valencia is beautiful and very hot. I have met the most marvellous man, Luiz Felipe Santoro. He is working at an incredible hotel here called the Hotel San

Sebastian. We're very in love—he's my soul mate,'" Nell recited, staring daggers at the Spaniard who had so far not even had the decency to look embarrassed.

"'I can hardly believe it myself but we've decided to get married as soon as possible.'" At this point Nell's voice broke and she added bitterly, 'I suppose you know she's only on a gap year and has been travelling around Europe for the last six months. She's got a brilliant future, a scholarship to university…'

He arched a brow and sounded politely interested. 'No, I didn't know.'

A growling noise escaped Nell's throat before she squeezed her eyes shut and finished in a halting monotone. "'You'll love him as much as I do, or almost as much ha ha! I know you'll know the best way to break it to Mum and Dad. Love and kisses, Lucy.'"

She stuck out her chin, glared up at him and wished she didn't have such a height disadvantage. 'Well, what do you have to say now? Are you still denying it? Are you suggesting Lucy made it all up?'

'I'm impressed.'

Nell's self-righteous anger tilted over into confusion. He wasn't acting like a guilty man, but maybe he was one of those sociopaths you read about—the ones who had no moral compass, no values?

'Impressed by what?'

'You had a name of a hotel and my name and you found me. That is impressive.'

Nell gave a triumphant little cry of, 'So you admit it is you, then.' Before adding with feeling, 'It wasn't easy finding you.'

That was just about the understatement of the century. Her night flight had arrived at the airport very early for her to find that her luggage, such as it was, had ended up somewhere else. The people at the snooty hotel where she had stuck out like a sore thumb beside the affluent and well-dressed guests had been very uncooperative, if not damned rude, when she had mentioned Luiz Felipe Santoro. They clearly intended taking his home address to their graves.

If it hadn't been for the sweet fatherly doorman who had chased after her and suggested she might find the man she was looking for at the Castillo d'Oro her search might have stopped right there.

The only hire car she had been able to afford had no air conditioning and to top it all she'd got lost three times on the way to the castillo. The distance on the map was deceptive. Although quite close to the Mediterranean, the historic *estancia* set high on a lush plateau in the Sierra Nevada was not easy to reach.

It had been the day from hell and only a determination to save her niece from making a terrible mistake had kept Nell going.

And all the time at the back of her mind there had been the question, what if all this was pointless? What if Lucy had already married her Spaniard?

'Tell me,' she pleaded, catching hold of his jacket sleeve. 'Are you married?'

Something dark, bleak and very forbidding flickered into his eyes. For a moment Nell thought he was not going to reply.

'I was, but not now.'

Oh, my God. Lucy had not only got involved with an older man, she had got involved with an older man who already had a failed marriage behind him, and if his manner when he spoke of it was anything to go by the break up had not been amicable. But then he did not strike Nell as the sort of man who would shrug off a divorce and say, 'Let's stay good friends.'

'You're a resourceful woman.'

'I'm a woman who is fast running out of patience.' Nell, pleased at the crisp delivery, tilted her chin to a 'don't mess with me' angle. 'I want to see Lucy and I want to see her now. I don't know what your job is here, but I can't imagine your employers will be too impressed if I tell them what you've been up to!'

'Are you threatening me?'

'Yes!' And not doing a very good job of it. It was difficult to imagine a man looking less threatened than Lucy's lover... She grimaced—*Lucy's lover.* That sounded so wrong on so many levels!

On the silly and shallow level it hardly seemed fair her teenage niece was now officially more sexually experienced than she was.

'I do not work here.'

Nell, who suddenly realised she still had hold of his arm, regarded him with suspicion. 'You're a guest at this hotel?' She gave a tiny gasp of relief when her fingers finally responded to the message from her brain and let go. The impression of hard, lean strength lingered even when she rubbed her hand against the canvas bag slung around her neck.

'Not a guest, and not a hotel—this is the home of my grandmother, Doña Elena Santoro.'

The colour faded from her cheeks as Nell turned her head and stared at the vast Castillo d'Oro, a fortified stone edifice—a real castle complete with turrets.

'You live here?' That explained the superior attitude and the faint air of disdain, the man obviously considered anyone who didn't own a castle beneath him. Well, she for one was not impressed by inherited wealth.

She shook her head, not waiting for his confirmation, and said firmly, 'That doesn't change anything.'

'I'm not the man you're looking for. I've never met your niece.'

Frustrated and tired, tears springing to her eyes, Nell, who rarely cried, blinked angrily.

'I don't believe you!' She struggled not to, because if he was telling the truth she was no nearer finding Lucy than she had been this morning.

'But I do know the man you're looking for.'

Nell looked at him with a mixture of hope and suspicion.

'Come indoors and I'll explain.'

'I'm not going anywhere. I'm not budging from this spot!' Nell said, folding her arms across her chest.

'Have it your way, but I wouldn't like to have your epidermis tomorrow.' He glanced up at the relentlessly blue sky, then back at her face. 'You have the sort of fair skin that burns.' A slightly distracted expression drifted across his face as he stared at the pale curve of her throat.

'And freckles,' Nell murmured with a sigh.

The comment seemed to wake him from his reverie. Possibly he was feeling the heat too, Nell thought, noticing the bands of high colour that attracted her eye to the slashing contours of his marvellous high cheekbones.

CHAPTER THREE

THE dull pain drumming in her temples intensified as Nell watched him stroll back to the castillo not pausing even once to look back. He was so damned sure that she'd follow him the way women had no doubt been following him all his adult life—not that she would be following him in the same sense.

She would have loved to have the luxury of calling his bluff, but that gesture would have been pretty self-defeating. If he was speaking the truth and he knew who Lucy was with she had no choice but to follow him. And his point about the heat was valid; the protective factor of the moisturiser she had used that morning had to have worn off hours ago.

The cool inside the stone-walled castle was sheer bliss after the oppressive heat of the Valencian sun. She hurried, her feet echoing on the stone floors, to catch up with him.

'So who is the man?' Nell asked, trotting to pass him.

She turned and came to an abrupt halt. He had to follow suit or fall over her. He didn't do that, but he did get awfully close—close enough for her to receive a pretty hefty jolt as she got too close to the raw sexual aura he projected.

It passed through her body like an electrical current and was the weirdest and most disturbing thing that had ever happened to her. She pressed a hand to her heaving chest and hoped that he attributed her breathless condition to a lack of fitness combined with the altitude.

He glanced down, his dark eyes skimming her face. 'My cousin.'

Nell opened her mouth to demand more information when he placed a hand on the wall above her head. Nell closed her eyes and edged closer to panic as he leaned into her, his big body curling over her. She held her breath, then released it a moment later as she found herself pushed through a door behind her and into a big, light, airy room.

'Sit down. I'll order some refreshments.'

Nell ignored the offer—a pretty pointless defiance considering her knees were literally shaking. 'Your cousin?' Was he just trying to wriggle out of it? Send her off on a false trail?

'It fits. He had a holiday job at the hotel you spoke of. I arranged it for him myself.'

She still wasn't convinced. 'What about the name?'

'We were both christened Luiz Felipe. This is not the first time confusion has arisen, but it is the most…amusing.'

'You're both called Luiz Felipe.'

'I know—an appalling lack of imagination. We were both named after our grandfather, but in the family we call him Felipe usually.'

'So how old is this cousin of yours?' Nell's feelings were mixed. While she was obviously relieved that Lucy hadn't got mixed up with this man—hopefully his cousin was not the similar type of predatory male—it did mean that she still had no idea where Lucy was.

'I'm not sure.' He arched a brow. 'Eighteen, nineteen?'

Nell stared. 'You're asking me? Just how many cousins do you have?'

Luiz leaned his elbow on the mantel of the carved stone fireplace and moved a heavy candlestick with his forefinger. His air of preoccupation incensed Nell.

'I'm sorry if I'm boring you.'

The acid observation swung Luiz's attention back to the figure standing there with her hands planted on her slim hips. 'Sorry.' He produced a grin that had no hint of apology in it and answered her question. 'Just the one.'

'And you don't know how old he is?'

'We are not what you would call close.'

'But he's your cousin.' She searched his dark face for any sign he was being facetious and found none. 'Your family.'

'Families are all different and I think you will find that my attitude to family is one that more people could readily identify with than your own.'

Nell looked at him, appalled. 'Don't you care if your cousin ruins his life?'

'A person learns by their mistakes. Perhaps your niece will learn from hers?'

The odd inflection in his deep voice that made Nell wonder what his mistakes had been was absent as he added flippantly, 'And who am I to stand in the way of true love?'

Nell, her eyes narrowed, did not bother to disguise her utter disgust as she glared at him. 'Ha. The truth is you don't give a damn about anyone else. You're utterly and totally selfish—you've no intention of lifting a finger to stop your cousin making the biggest mistake of his life because you're utterly self-centred.'

She was midway through accusing him of possessing no family feeling when Ramon's joke came back to Luiz. The future Mrs Santoro! His lips curled into a wry smile that faded as he recognised the element of truth in Ramon's joke—a bride would be his grandmother's most precious birthday present.

Luiz was inclined initially to reject the crazy, though intriguing, idea forming in his head, because it was so obviously, well...*crazy*. He could not pinpoint the exact moment that it stopped being crazy but actually almost logical, but suddenly he found himself asking—*Why not?*

He would never be able to give his grandmother the wife and heir she longed for him to provide, so wasn't this an alternative where nobody got hurt? Why *shouldn't* he be studying the flushed and angry face of the future Mrs Santoro? It could work.

Why wait for her birthday?

There were always two ways of looking at a situation. Some people would think his idea a moment of inspiration while others would think it a moment of madness.

Luiz didn't care about the label, he just cared about the result.

'I have a proposition to put to you.'

Nell regarded him with an expression of baffled frustration. He had not even attempted to defend himself. She wasn't even sure if he had heard a word she had said.

'I know where they are.'

Her eyes widened. 'Lucy and your cousin?'

He nodded.

'So where…?'

He pushed aside the poignant image of the cottage by the sea where he and Rosa had lived and held up a hand to stop her. Fulfilling his side of the bargain he was proposing would mean him going there for the first time in many years. The first time since Rosa died.

'First you need to do something for me.'

He saw the alarm flare in her eyes and sketched a cynical grin. 'Relax, not *that* something. You're really not my type.'

As if to challenge his careless contention the image that formed in his head of one perfect breast fitting perfectly into his hand momentarily vaporised every other thought.

'Imagine my devastation,' she snarled, irrationally deflated. 'Forget the dramatic pause and get to the point—what do I have to do?'

'Come and meet my grandmother.'

Nell's face fell. 'That's it?' Obviously there was a catch.

'And go along with whatever I say.'

'But I don't understand why—?'

He cut across her with an autocratic shake of his dark head. There was no time for a question and answer session. If he paused long enough to think about this he strongly suspected that he'd bail.

'I do not require you to understand. As I said, I simply require you to go along with anything I say—no matter what it is.'

'But why?'

'Do you want to find the lovers?'

Nell's expression reflected her dilemma. 'Oh, all right, then.' What choice did she have? 'And afterwards you'll tell me where they are.'

'*Querida,*' he promised with a grin, 'I'll take you to them. Shake on it.'

Nell dragged her eyes away from the magnetic pull of his deep-set dark eyes and regarded the hand he held towards her for a long moment before finally extending her own.

As his cool fingers closed around hers Nell tried to ignore the warning voice in her head that told her she was making a big mistake.

It was a lot more difficult to ignore the prickle under her skin that had nothing to do with sunburn and a lot to do with their brief physical contact.

CHAPTER FOUR

THE castle was a maze. Nell followed Luiz for what felt like miles along stone-floored corridors before he finally halted.

'This is my grandmother's room.' Luiz reached for the door and stopped. 'Wait here. I will be back presently.'

Left with little choice but to obey his terse instruction, Nell began to study the large tapestry of brilliant colours on the wall opposite.

The battle scene it portrayed was nothing compared to the one being waged in her head. *Just what are you doing, Nell? This is crazy, totally crazy. You don't know this man—you don't even know what you've agreed to and who's to say he will keep his word?*

Before she could totally lose her nerve Luiz Santoro returned. Without a word he took her left hand and slid a ring onto her finger.

'What are you doing? What…w-what is that?' she stammered, staring at her finger. The gold band felt heavy, a rose-coloured diamond surrounded by what she assumed were rubies in an antique setting.

She was no expert but it didn't look like the sort of thing you found in a Christmas cracker.

He lifted his brows. 'A ring.'

'I can see that,' she retorted crankily. 'What is it doing on my finger?'

'Window dressing.'

'For what?'

'That is not relevant.'

Nell shook her head and dug in her heels literally. 'I'm not taking another step until you explain this thing.' She waved the offending jewellery him.

Luiz studied her mutinous face for a moment, then gave a philosophical shake of his head. 'My grandmother—'

'The one who owns this house?'

His dark brows twitched into a straight line of disapproval at the interruption. 'The one who own this house and the *estancia* it stands upon. She is ill…maybe…'

He paused, unwilling to voice the possibility, as if saying the thing made it more likely to happen. He was impatient with the lack of logic in his thought processes, but then when you cared for a person it was hard to always be logical.

He glanced down at the young woman who was staring up at him, suspicion and wariness reflected in her clear eyes, and thought, Logic does not feature in that glossy head at any level…just neat emotion.

It made her a frustrating person to negotiate with.

'Maybe?' Nell prompted.

'Maybe even dying.'

Nell's face dropped. 'I'm sorry.' It was hard to tell from his stony expression if her sympathy was either required or desired.

Not that the lack of emotion in his features meant he didn't have any, she reminded herself. Give the man the benefit of the doubt—she had not cried at her father's funeral or, for that matter, since. Pushing aside the thought, Nell focused on his dark face—too much focus because she immediately started to feel dizzy.

'We all die, and my grandmother is eighty-five.'

Nell found the clinical pronouncement chilling, but not as chilling as the total lack of feeling in his voice or manner. She suspected he didn't deserve the benefit of any doubt—the man was just plain cold.

'I'm sorry your grandmother is ill, but that still doesn't explain the ring—' she waved her hand in an expansive gesture '—or any of this.'

'It is her wish that I marry and provide an heir.'

Nell, her eyes wide—she was clearly dealing with someone who was delusional and possibly dangerous—started to shake her head and back away.

'I care about Lucy, but if you think I'm going to…m-m…' She shook her head again. 'Some sacrifices I'm not willing to make. Let her leave the place to this other Luiz Felipe—he seems more than willing to marry.' And for all she knew provide heirs! 'God, I really need to find Lucy.'

For a split second he looked perplexed by her response. 'Sacrifice? You think…?' He threw back his dark head and laughed, a deep attractive sound. 'I am not asking you to marry me, and Felipe would not make a suitable custodian for the *estancia*.'

Nell pursed her lips, perversely irritated that he appeared to find the idea so hilarious. 'So you don't want a wife.'

His expression sobered and she glimpsed something that wasn't cold calculation flicker at the back of his eyes. It was stark, shocking pain.

'I had a wife. I require no one to fill her place in my life or heart.'

Did that mean the ex-wife had walked…? The image of him as broken-hearted, discarded husband was one Nell's imagination just wouldn't expand to accommodate. Actually she felt a lot more comfortable believing he didn't have a heart at all, let alone a bruised one, so she changed the subject.

'So you think you'd be a...*suitable custodian?* Is that shorthand for you fancy yourself as king of the castle?' He certainly had the regal manner. 'So you don't mind if your cousin gets the girl but not the money.'

'There is no money.'

Nell rolled her eyes. 'Sure there isn't.' She folded her arms across her chest and challenged, 'So, if you don't have an avaricious bone in your body—' gorgeous body '—why this silliness?' she finished, thinking she might well ask herself the same question. Stop drooling, Nell!

'My grandmother raised me, she has taught me everything I know, I owe her everything and I wish her to die a happy woman.'

'But...'

His eyes flashed as he frowned in exasperation and mimed a zipping motion across his mouth. 'Will you be silent and let me finish?'

Nell's chin went up as she viewed him, eyes narrowed in dislike. 'If you get to the point.'

'My grandmother is a redoubtable woman. She has carried the burden of running the *estancia* alone for many years. She was a young woman when her husband died. She does not want that for me. She wants me to be happy and she believes that for that I need a...' he paused, his lips twisting into a cynical smile before he completed '...soul mate, a wife.'

'Me? No way!'

'My thought exactly.'

'And I'm not lying for you.'

'I'm not asking you to. I'm hoping that the ring will do the trick.'

'But what if she doesn't...?' Nell gave an awkward grimace.

'Die,' he inserted, turning his head so that Nell could not see the muscle he could feel clenching in his cheek. 'It is possible,' he conceded. 'She is tough and she has been ill before. If that happens…' nothing in Luiz's demeanour suggested how desperately he clung to that hope as he calmly outlined his hastily formed fall-back strategy '…I will simply explain that you have been forced to return to England. Long-distance love affairs are notoriously difficult and ours will die a natural death, possibly due, I think, to your infidelity.'

Nell stared. She almost believed it herself! 'You seem to have thought of everything.'

He took her comment as a compliment and bowed his head in acknowledgement. 'I have that reputation.' And whether it was deserved or not it made him feared by his competitors.

That was not entirely a bad thing in the cutthroat world he operated in. A man used every advantage he had, and one advantage Luiz no longer had was the element of surprise that had enabled him as an unknown twenty-year-old to make his first million before the competition had become aware of his existence.

Now they knew he was there, but he enjoyed a challenge.

'Maybe you've actually convinced yourself that you're doing this to make her happy because you're ashamed to admit how far you'd go to make sure you inherit this place?'

Luiz Santoro looked almost as shocked as Nell felt to hear her private speculation voiced out loud.

She took an involuntary step back as eyes that housed sheer molten rage connected with her own. Before she had a chance to be defensive or even sensibly scared it was gone, leaving her wondering if it had ever been there at all.

Luiz, on the point of ramming his financial success down her superior, self-righteous little throat, stopped himself. Why justify his actions to this girl, when he never justified himself to anyone?

Her opinion of him was of no consequence but defending himself would force him to question this.

'You need not trouble yourself with my motivation or my

self-delusion, just look sweet and in love,' he mocked, placing a finger under her chin.

Nell, her pulse racing and no longer just from fear, held herself rigid while he studied her upturned features. 'You don't look in love.' He sounded irritated by the discovery.

She pushed his hand away and directed her darting glance at some point behind him. Don't panic, Nell—you can leave at any time you like. He can't stop you.

All you have to do is walk away.

'That's because I'm not.' She ran her tongue nervously across her dry lips and said, 'This is all too weird. I need time. I've changed my mind. I think—'

'Not an option.'

Without any warning at all he bent his head and pressed his mouth to hers.

The hot, hungry kiss did not start slow and build; it was hard, demanding, and began at a mind-blowing level of intimacy that nothing could have prepared her for. As his mouth moved with innate sensuality across her own the heat flared inside her and her senses were flooded with the texture and taste of him.

At the first erotic stabbing incursion of his tongue her insides dissolved and something inside her snapped. Suddenly she was kissing him back, her fingers spread out across his hard chest as she groaned into his mouth and pressed her body into his, responding to a frantic need to be closer.

When Luiz lifted his head he looked as dazed as she felt, but maybe she had imagined it because a second later he was removing her hands from his chest and pushing her through the door ahead of him.

'And don't think,' he said in her ear.

Nell, her mind still numb with shock, thought, Walk away! But her will seemed to have deserted her, her body was nailed to the spot with shock.

Struggling to prove she still had a mind of her own…God, I kissed him back…she flashed him a killer look. 'If you do that again I will make you regret it!' she snapped.

Luiz, who was already regretting the impulsive action, did not respond. He looked at her lush lips and thought about the way she had tasted. Then he pushed the thought away. For a man who prided himself on his iron control it should have been a simple matter.

It wasn't.

A man could not excel at everything and it was clear that he was not good at spontaneity…especially spontaneity that involved this woman.

Resentment and humiliation swirled through Nell's veins. Calculatingly, he'd done that to shut her up and get her through the door and the worst part was it had worked!

And while she was reduced to a shell-shocked wreck by a simple kiss—just a kiss, what was wrong with her?—he was acting, it seemed to a mortified Nell, as if nothing had happened! I kissed him back!

Nell stumbled a little and his hand shot out to steady her and stayed at her elbow. She did not mistake the gesture for concern. He's probably getting ready to rugby tackle me to the ground if I try and run, she thought.

A rugby tackle would have been infinitely preferable to a kiss…although rolling on the ground with him did present some worrying opportunities for making a fool of herself.

The room they entered was in shadow. Nell could make out the general outline of furniture and a frail figure propped up in a big carved bed. She spoke in Spanish but Luiz replied in English.

'Surprise? I doubt it. Don't tell me the jungle drums have not already told you I had arrived.'

Nell tried to slow her laboured breathing as she watched Luiz walk towards the bed and bend over it.

Seeing the walking frame beside the bed brought back a rush of memories and to her horror Nell felt her eyelids prickle with tears. Eight weeks and I cry now. Please, no, not now. Inch by inch she fought her way back to control, dabbing angrily at the moisture at the corners of her eyes.

'I've brought you a visitor and she doesn't speak Spanish.'

The contrast between his callous attitude to her moments earlier and the tenderness in his manner as he kissed the sunken cheek of the tiny figure lying in the bed increased the emotional ache in her throat. She remained stubbornly reluctant to endow him with finer feelings or motives, but if he didn't love this old lady he was a very good actor.

'This is Nell.'

How could anyone put so much expression into one word—one name?

It was astonishing, and her reaction to the warm husky intonation in his deep voice suggesting unspoken intimacies was no less shocking.

Luiz reached a hand towards her and she responded without thinking to the compelling message in his eyes and stepped forward, taking his hand. An embarrassing rush of heat passed through Nell's body as he tugged her towards him and slipped his arm around her waist before pulling her into his body.

She suddenly felt a spasm of sympathy for Lucy. If his cousin had half this man's seductive powers, then it was hardly surprising that her inexperienced niece had fallen so hard.

'Turn that light on, Luiz.'

Nell blinked as the light from an angle lamp fell across her face.

'Good bones...' came the verdict. The sharp eyes slid thoughtfully back to her grandson's face, before she returned her attention to Nell. 'Not your usual type, Luiz.'

Tell me something I don't know, thought Nell as to her relief Luiz aimed the light away from her eyes. Then prompted by the expression in his eyes, she held out her hand. Like some sort of puppet, observed the disgusted voice in her head.

'Well, now I won't have to change my will, Luiz,' Doña Elena joked.

It took a couple of seconds for Nell to register the comment, and when she did she was gripped by a wave of disillusionment. She had wanted to know and now there was no doubt. It was quite irrational to feel so let down. People did unpleasant, low, nasty things when large sums of money were involved, so why should he be any different?

'Were you going to leave it to Felipe?'

The standing joke between them raised a weak smile from the old lady and a horrified look from Nell. Elena Santoro, who was perfectly aware that her younger grandson had no fondness for the *estancia* that was, to quote him, '*an anachronism in the modern world*', teased back.

'Possibly.' Felipe had even less enthusiasm for the responsibilities that came with it and he remained mystified by their grandmother's stubborn determination to hang onto what he referred to as a damned money pit. He had been almost comically relieved when she had explained to him that it was her intention his cousin would inherit, but he would have her house in Seville and the art collection it contained.

Turning her head towards Nell, she asked, 'You have met Felipe?'

Nell shook her head. 'Not yet.' She could *almost* feel sorry for him.

'He is a good boy, artistic, but I expect he will grow out of that. You notice I do not speak of my sons. If I left the *estancia* to them, Nell, they would split it up and sell it off to speculators before I was cold in my grave.' She broke off as her slight frame was racked by hacking coughs. 'I'm fine, don't fuss, Luiz,' she gasped breathlessly as she patted away his solicitous hand. 'So when, Nell, are you going to marry my grandson?'

Luiz spoke for her. 'We have not set a date yet.'

Despite her physical frailty there was nothing weak about the glare that was directed at Luiz. 'Does the girl not have a voice, Luiz? Let her speak,' she quavered imperiously.

Nell lifted her chin. If Luiz was scared about what she might say, he ought to be. 'I can speak.' She flashed Luiz a look of distaste and thought, Let him sweat.

'Tell me about yourself.'

It was a request, not an order, but Nell was starting to realise this was not a lady who did requests.

'What would you like to know? I'm twenty-five, a library assistant.'

'How did Luiz come to meet an English library assistant?'

'Perhaps it was fated.'

Luiz gave an enigmatic smile and smoothed Nell's hair back from her brow as though, she thought as she fought the impulse to pull away, he had performed the tender act a hundred times before. You had to admire the man's acting ability, if not his morals.

The old lady returned her attention to Nell and almost caught her rolling her eyes. 'You have family?'

'I have a sister and a brother, both older and both married with children.'

'You live alone?'

'I live with my dad,' she said without thinking. Then she remembered and muttered, 'So stupid, I keep forgetting. I *lived* with Dad.'

'Your father died?'

Luiz, noticing for the first time the violet smudges beneath her big eyes, felt an unidentifiable emotion break loose inside him as she pressed the heels of her hands into her eyes and scrubbed them like a child before responding to his grandmother's question.

'Eight weeks ago.' Beside her she was conscious of Luiz stiffening.

'Eight weeks,' she repeated in a softer, almost surprised voice. Weeks that had been filled with practicalities; there had been no time for grieving.

Lots of practicalities, she mused, thinking of the pile of packing cases she had left when she had jumped on the first flight available. The removals people would be arriving in the morning and there would be no one to let them in.

And Clare, who was arriving to collect the more valuable pieces of furniture that she had claimed for her own home, was going to be annoyed. Nell was conscious that the idea of her sister's anger and the removal people standing on the doorstep ought to bother her more, but it didn't.

'The house was only on the market a week when it sold.' You are telling them this why, Nell? 'It would have been too big for me anyway.'

Clare and Paul had both said it was fine by them if she stayed on for a while, but she knew they had both been pleased when she had put the property straight on the market. They would both find the money from the sale useful. And as they had said, she could find a nice little place of her own.

'Your father, he had been ill for a long time, Nell?' There was a gentler note than she had yet heard in the old lady's voice.

Nell nodded tiredly and registered Luiz say something that sounded angry in Spanish. His grandmother responded, saying, 'Can't you see she needs to talk? The little one has been bottling up her emotions.'

'He had a stroke. It left him partially paralyzed down his left side...' Nell sketched an explanatory sweeping motion down her side. 'He had some mobility problems so I didn't go to university.'

If she had taken her university place and not stayed on the option would have been a nursing home or sheltered accommodation and Nell knew how much her dad loved his home. And with a few modifications to the house he had become reasonably independent, to the point that before his death he had been pushing for Nell to go to college as a mature student.

'But he was doing really well. That's why it was such a shock when he…' Her voice trailed away as she swallowed past the lump in her throat. 'It was pneumonia.'

Nell heard her voice crack and thought, Please, no, not now, not here. Her grief lay lodged like an icy block in her chest. When it melted she knew there would be a lot of moisture and a lot of pain—but not now.

Luiz, watching as she forced her stiff features into a composed smile, felt her grief as a physical pain in his chest.

'I told him that it was my choice to stay at home. I wanted to be there with him. There was no need for him to feel guilty about university, but…'

Nell didn't connect herself with the strangled whimper. The second sob she felt as it worked its way up from deep down inside her and escaped and then she couldn't stop them.

As the tears began to flow she turned her head and found Luiz's chest. A hand came up to hold her there and another wrapped around her ribs, hauling her up against him.

'This was not a good idea,' Luiz, his face set like stone, said to his grandmother as he cradled her shaking body. The sound of her sobs tore him up inside; he had never felt so impotent in his life, or more responsible.

He should, he told himself, have recognised her vulnerability, but he hadn't and this was the result.

He rested his chin on the top of Nell's head and rocked her in his arms. 'It will be all right,' he soothed.

'The girl has a sense of duty. I like that.'

'I think she's had enough,' he said abruptly, before he swept her casually into his arms and walked out of the room with her.

CHAPTER FIVE

NELL'S sobs went straight to an unprotected portion of Luiz's heart. Each sob seemed to be dragged from deep inside her. It was painful to listen to, to feel as they racked her body.

While she wept Sabina floated silently into the room, took in the scene at a glance and, after nodding at him, left. When she returned a short time later she was carrying a tray laden with sandwiches and cake, a coffee pot and two cups.

Luiz, nodding as she left, would not have minded the addition of something more stimulating. It was not a need he felt when facing the collapse of a multimillion-dollar deal, but right now... He glanced down and winced. It seemed to him the tears would never stop. But gradually, over the next few minutes, to his relief they lessened until she gave a final deep, shuddering sigh and lifted her head from his shoulder, her damp cheek brushing his as she did so.

He made no attempt to stop her as she slid to the opposite end of the sofa.

Weak in the aftermath of the emotional excesses, Nell lifted her hand to push away the damp skein of hair that had flopped into her eyes.

'I'm sorry,' she muttered, not looking at him.

It bothered her that she had lost control, but for some

reason it bothered her a lot more that she had lost control in front of this man of all people.

'I'm fine now.' Her level look dared him to contradict her.

'Of course you are,' he said, pushing a box of tissues supplied by the ever-alert Sabina her way.

'About your father—'

Nell blew her nose. 'I don't want to talk about it,' she said in a fierce little voice. 'You've got what you want.'

Luiz, on whom her unfriendly attitude had not been wasted, angled a questioning brow. 'I have?'

'Well, your grandmother's going to leave you her loot, isn't she?' She lifted her scornful red-rimmed eyes to his and added, 'I suppose it beats working for a living.'

A look she couldn't interpret crossed his face. It wasn't guilt, but it should have been.

'Perhaps we do not all have your strong moral integrity.'

The faint derision she heard in his voice brought an angry flush to Nell's tear-stained face. 'I'm not suggesting I'm perfect.'

Luiz looked at her, the red swollen eyes, the pink nose, and found himself thinking, Maybe not perfect, but awfully appealing. And not his type…even his grandmother had recognised this.

She sniffed and he experienced a sharp twinge of emotion. Refusing to recognise its source, he got abruptly to his feet and walked across to the table where the tea tray lay undisturbed.

'Can I get something for you?'

'You can get me Lucy, take me to her.'

He regarded her incredulously. 'Now?'

'Certainly now.'

He shook his head doubtfully. 'You don't look in any condition to go anywhere.'

'Yeah, well, I'm terribly sorry I don't reach your standard of airbrushed perfection, but we had a deal and I've done my bit, which, I have to tell you, has left a nasty taste in my mouth, so now it's your turn. Do you actually even know where they are? If so just tell me. I'll drive myself there—I have a car.'

The silence stretched. She was, he decided, more than capable of doing just that if he allowed her. The woman gave a new meaning to stubborn…or maybe, he conceded, she just had to keep going because if she stopped or slowed down she would feel. The grief would come crashing in. It was a coping mechanism that he recognised, he had used it after Rosa died. In his case it had taken the form of work and more work that had been viewed in some quarters as a lack of caring.

Not that Luiz had cared. Strange that back then he had been unconcerned what anyone thought, and now Nell's assumption he was an avaricious scrounger felt like a slap in the face. It had been a warped sense of pride that had prevented him putting her right, warped because he had given her little reason to have a good opinion of him—a good opinion he still refused to accept he wanted.

'The road, such as it is, is not good. Only a four-wheel drive or preferably a horse will get you there.'

'I don't ride a horse.' But it was not difficult to see Luiz Santoro on one.

'Then four-wheel drive it is.'

Nell gave a watery smile of relief. 'You'll take me?'

'As you are clearly not fit to be let out alone—yes, I will.'

Nell let the inference she needed a keeper pass. She was just so relieved to actually be doing something and not standing around.

He glanced at the metallic banded watch on his wrist, screwed up his eyes as though making a mental calculation, and said, 'I have some things to attend to, so we'll say an hour's time. In the meantime eat. I'll send Sabina, who will show you where to go if you want to freshen up.'

His frowning scrutiny brought a self-conscious flush to Nell's face. The last thing she wanted was to look in a mirror.

'Who is Sabina?' she began, but he had gone.

She did not have long to wait to find out as the Spanish woman appeared moments later carrying fresh coffee. Nell found her manner soothing as she explained in heavily accented but perfect English that she was the housekeeper.

A few sandwiches forced down, her caffeine levels topped up, her hair combed and her face washed, Nell felt a lot more like herself and able to cope...*so long as she didn't think of that kiss.*

Luiz returned forty-five minutes later.

He had been to his grandmother's sick room to explain he would be away for the rest of the day.

It was soon clear that his plan had gone even better than he had anticipated. His grandmother had been more animated than he had seen her in many weeks.

Listening to her talk about his English bride, and the grandchildren she looked forward to living long enough to see born, made him wonder if extricating himself from this fake betrothal should the need arise might not be as simple as he had predicted.

It was a problem of his own making and, ironically, one he sincerely hoped he would have to face. But though the future was still uncertain and he could not allow himself to hope, one thing was clear: Nell Frost had Doña Elena's stamp of approval. Nell Frost, who was nowhere to be seen.

Luiz looked at the disturbed tray, and glanced around the room seeing no immediate signs of the blonde English girl. Noticing that the double doors that led into the library were wide open, he strolled through them and almost immediately found her, perched on the top steps of one of the ladders that gave access to the topmost shelves that lined the room.

Lost in a book, she did not notice his entrance and Luiz did not immediately make her aware of his presence. Instead he paused—she made an aesthetically pleasing picture, the sun filtering through the wooden shutters that covered the south-facing library windows revealing not only the golden highlights in her hair, but a great deal of the slender curves beneath the cotton dress that it rendered virtually transparent.

His response to the image was more earthy than aesthetic.

Irritated, he had to make a conscious effort to put his libido back in its box. There was a time and a place for such indulgences and this was neither… It seemed a good moment to remind himself that she was not even his type!

He liked tall, athletically built women and she barely reached his shoulder, he recalled as his glance slid down her slim bare legs.

His hooded lids came down. Not close to his type, he reminded himself.

'A busman's holiday?'

She jumped at the sound of his voice and slid the dusty tome balanced on her knee into the vacant space on the top shelf. She did it with the care such a rare treasure deserved, which gave her the time to gather the wits that had gone walkabout the moment she had heard his voice.

She cleared her throat and pitched her voice at a cool level, ignoring the shivery tremors in her stomach as she told him, 'I was looking at your books.' The book she had extracted had been the only one Nell felt able to touch without protective gloves and yet still would have been counted a gem in many collections.

Did he know, she wondered, just how many rare and precious books this room held?

'Could you not have looked at them on ground level?'

Nell ignored the question. 'Do you realise that there is no system here at all?'

His brows rose at the admonitory heat in her voice.

'There are some incredibly rare books here.'

'And it's a great shame they belong to an unappreciative philistine?'

'You said it.'

'I believe my great-grandfather was something of a collector.' Over the years he had suggested to his grandmother that the collection be catalogued, but she had considered the project a costly waste of money.

Nell's indignation flared. That someone so uninformed should have access to such a treasure seemed sacrilege.

'Well, he'll be turning in his grave right now because the condition of some…' She made a clicking noise of disapproval with her tongue and shook her head. 'Actually it's *criminal*. There are some incredibly rare—'

Luiz's amused drawl cut across her animated protest. 'I have rarely seen a woman display such passion for anything unless it is a designer handbag.'

Nell couldn't let the sexist comment pass unchallenged. 'Really, if the women you know only get excited by handbags it speaks volumes for your skill in bed, and,' she added, thinking of her limited collection at home, 'you probably know more about designer handbags than I do.'

Her satisfaction at delivering the cutting comeback lasted for the two seconds it took her brain to supply an image of tumbled sheets and entwined limbs, fair skin looking very pale against the dark.

It had been clearly a major error to introduce the subject of the bedroom when she was talking to this man. Nell squeezed her eyes tightly shut against the explicit mental images playing in her head.

'I didn't mean—' To mentally undress you.

'To issue a challenge?'

She opened her mouth to protest but before she could offer

a hasty placatory reply he added, 'Or cast a slur on my masculinity…' There was something mingled with the sardonic amusement that sent a shivery surge of sensation along her nerve endings. In her eagerness to deny the suggestion Nell almost fell off her perch as she shook her head vigorously in horrified denial.

'Be careful!'

His sharp warning echoed the voice in her own head, though the voice in her head was not so worried about falling off the ladder as the knot of excitement pulsing low in her belly!

Good God, Nell, get a grip, girl! This is what happens when you don't have a life. You step outside your comfort zone and the first OK male you see makes your hormones go haywire.

Nell's darting eyes connected for a split second with the dark gleaming gaze of the man below and a small sigh of alarm left her lips as adrenaline and desire surged through her. She drew back, her brows knitting in consternation as she shuffled her bottom back along the top step until she could feel the spines of the books dig into her back.

All right, better than OK.

She took a couple of calming deep breaths and injected a note of amusement into her voice as she leaned forward, her hair swinging like a bell around her face.

'Truth told, I'm more interested in finding Lucy than exploring your male insecurities.'

'Don't worry, I'm not that insecure.'

That was the problem, she thought.

'Are you planning on coming down from there any time soon?'

In response to the question Nell gave a small shriek, drawn from her lips as her foot slipped. 'Oops,' she said as she grabbed at the rail to steady herself.

Below her she heard him growl something in husky Spanish that didn't sound polite—not polite but very sexy.

She made the rest of her descent more carefully until three steps from the ground a pair of big hands spanned her waist.

'What do you think you're doing?' Set safely on the floor, she spun around pink-cheeked and indignant.

'Preventing a potential accident.'

The cool explanation drew a derisive snort from Nell, or it would have if her choppy breathing had allowed anything but a faint sigh to emerge from her parted lips.

'You shouldn't climb ladders, Miss Frost, if you have no head for heights.'

Very conscious that his hands were still resting lightly on her waist, Nell lifted her chin and brushed a shiny skein of hair from her face.

To her intense relief Luiz's hands fell away, but he was still standing close enough for her to feel the heat from his lean body.

'Actually I have no problem with heights.' Tall Spaniards with fallen angel faces were another matter.

She struggled to tear her eyes from the sternly sensual outline of his wide mobile mouth and cleared her throat as she recalled his kiss.

'It's these shoes.' She glanced down at her sensible shoes and Luiz followed the direction of her gaze. 'The soles have no grip.'

More of a grip than she had, she reflected with a small grimace of self-disgust. It was a struggle to keep focused and concentrate. Her mind kept drifting off on dangerous tangents.

And you're not the sort of girl who has sexual fantasies, she reminded herself as she felt his steadying hand on her arm.

'You have very small feet.' Luiz's glance lifted, the distracted expression she saw in his eyes vanishing as he scanned her face and added in an accusing manner, 'Are you all right?'

She kept her eyes trained on the floor and lied through her teeth. 'Fine.' So the man was sexy—it wasn't as if she had some sort of uncontrollable sex drive.

Luiz watched as a warm tide of colour rose up her slender neck until her face was aglow with colour. Moments earlier she had been deadly pale. 'You don't look fine.'

Her chin came up, though she continued to dodge his gaze, studying a point over his left shoulder.

'I can't help the way I look.'

And he, Luiz realised with a sense of shock, could not help liking the ways she looked—a lot. He had not wanted more than sex from a woman in a long time, to do so now with a woman he barely knew felt like a betrayal to Rosa's memory. Not that there could be a comparison with his feelings now. Rosa had known him inside out and he her, they had grown up together and their bond had grown and blossomed.

'Well, are you ready?'

Nell responded to the grouchy enquiry with a robust reminder that she was the one who had been waiting.

CHAPTER SIX

THE big off-roader, unlike the car Nell had arrived in, was equipped with air-conditioning. She got in and Luiz immediately irritated her by telling her to fasten her seat belt as though, she reflected crankily, she were an imbecile or a small child.

To ignore him would unfortunately have proved she was at least one, so Nell fastened herself in.

'Where are we going?' A little late in the day to display this basic curiosity but better late than never.

He flashed her a quick sideways look. 'A cottage the other side of the mountain.' He nodded towards a blue-tinged peak that framed the castle. 'By the sea.'

'What makes you so sure that they are there?'

'Felipe has always liked the place. He has mentioned on more than one occasion it's his idea of the perfect love nest.'

Or lair, she thought darkly.

Luiz showed no further inclination to talk and a silence not of the comfortable variety stretched between them.

The road turned out to be as bad as he had suggested and the gradient steadily increased, until it became so steep the back wheels struggled to gain purchase on the potholed ground.

On one occasion Nell winced.

Luiz flashed a look at her pale, tense face and said, 'It's

not normally this bad—they had some freak storms up here last month.'

'So long as we don't have any now.' Not long later the road levelled out and they began to travel through a forested area. Nell expressed her surprise that there was so much greenery.

'Oak groves,' he said by way of explanation.

'Can't you go any faster?'

'I could,' he replied, not increasing his speed. Not necessarily a bad thing, Nell was forced to concede as they were taking a sharp bend that necessitated her clinging to the door to stop herself being thrown against him.

'You could drive, but it would require you to keep your eyes open.'

It would also require her mind not drifting off without warning and, while she was forced to share an enclosed space with him, that seemed unlikely. 'I'm not good with heights, and you should have your eyes on the road, not on me.'

'Perhaps I'm helpless in the face of your fatal allure.' Luiz's heavy lids lowered concealing the flicker of surprise at the unexpected truth in his dark eyes.

What was it about her face that fascinated him?

Luiz turned his head and allowed his eyes to slide across the soft contours of her profile before returning his attention to the road. He had never met a woman who had such an expressive face, who wore her emotions so close to the surface.

Rosa had been a classic beauty.

This girl was not; he felt a need to search out her imperfections. To the objective observer, her eyes were beautiful. The rest of her features were not exceptional, but her unexceptional mouth, far too generous for her small face, exerted a growing fascination for him. He kept hearing that husky sigh she had breathed into his mouth when she had melted into his arms.

His sarcasm shouldn't have hurt but it did.

'Very funny,' Nell said, flashing a cool smile before she turned her head and trained her eyes on the passing scenery.

Busy refusing to acknowledge the odd achy lump in her throat—she was just tired—it took a few minutes to register the mist rising off the ground. It hung low, shrouding the vegetation in a spectral white fog and reducing visibility.

'Will the fog get worse, do you think?'

'Possibly.' The fog would be the least of their problems, Luiz mused with a glance towards the fuel dial that hovered around empty.

He released a long hissing sigh of irritation through his clenched teeth. Only last summer he had given Felipe, who had just got his driving licence, a lecture when he had got stranded driving to a party at a friend's house.

His cousin would no doubt be amused to see the tables reversed, but he doubted that his driving companion would find the situation so amusing when she realised. For the last few miles the four-wheel drive had been running on fumes, dashing his earlier hopes they might make it to the coast before the tank ran dry. He saw no useful purpose in telling her—she would find out soon enough.

Struggling to see the funny side himself, Luiz flashed a sideways glance at her profile—any excuse. Her pensive profile, chin pressed into her white knuckles, smooth brow furrowed, was turned to the window. She looked tense enough to snap like an overstrung guitar. Luiz could almost see visible waves of tension and impatience rolling off her rigid body.

His reply regarding the weather was irritatingly vague but his confident manner did ease her anxiety slightly.

'Just why are you here?'

Nell cast him an irritated look. 'I've already explained.'

'Yes, I know you have to save your niece from the clutches of my cousin.' The idea of Felipe as some sort of serial seducer of innocence brought a wry smile to Luiz's lips. 'This,' he conceded drily, 'I know.'

Nell saw the smile and felt her anger surge.

'What I don't understand,' he continued, 'is why *you?*'

Nell shook her head in impatient bafflement. 'What do you mean, why me?'

'Well, does this niece of yours not have parents? Your brother or sister?'

Nell, who could see where he was going with this, gave a shrug. 'Lucy is my sister Clare's eldest.' Clare also had a new baby.

'So why does the task fall on your shoulders?'

'It was me that Lucy contacted. She wanted me to tell her parents.'

'But you didn't.'

Her lips tightened at the implied criticism she read in his comment. 'If I get to Lucy in time there won't be any need to worry them.'

'They are parents—worry is included in the job description.'

'And I'm only the aunt, you mean. It just so happens that Lucy and I are very close.' Nell heard the defensive note in her voice and frowned. Why was she explaining herself to him?

Maybe because she thought he might be right? Wasn't her reaction to the e-mail a bit over the top? Was this a rescue mission or was she running away?

Nell closed down the line of internal dialogue and gave a scornful sniff.

'I suppose you think I should just let her sink or swim?' The ice-queen expression was beginning to make her face ache.

'That was certainly an option. We learn by our mistakes.'

Nell regarded him with disgust. 'Are you saying you did— that at some point you have made a mistake? Imagine my shock—I thought you achieved infallibility in the cradle.' The only effect of her acid jibe was one of his trademark lopsided smiles.

The man had the hide of a rhino and he had probably been perfecting that smile to its full drop-dead gorgeous potency for the last ten years in a mirror.

'We're not all as tough as you are, Mr Santoro. Or as smug,' she added under her breath.

'I think you'd better make it Luiz while that ring is on your finger.'

Nell's eyes slid automatically to her finger where the rock that belonged in a bank vault or a museum sparkled. Without responding to his comment beyond a fulminating look of dislike directed at his hatefully perfect patrician profile, she began struggling to wrench it off her finger. There was after all no reason for the trappings of this now, with no one here to see it.

'The damn thing's stuck!' she panted. 'It won't budge an inch,' she wailed, still wrestling with the heavy ring.

His brows lifted. 'Don't worry, there's always amputation. There was also the option to tell the girl's parents, but you didn't.'

The change of subject caused Nell to stop struggling with the ring.

'This was their problem, not yours.'

'I've already explained they couldn't have done anything.' She had done the right thing, hadn't she...? Although a note to Clare might have been a good idea—my God, they might even be searching for me!

His brows lifted. 'But you can?'

Nell, her jaw tight, viewed him through the veil of her lashes. 'In case you've not noticed, I *am* doing something, always supposing you're right and they are in this cottage and I'm not too late.' She sucked in a startled breath and braced her arms to steady herself when without warning Luiz swerved to avoid a fallen branch that lay across the road.

Not by so much as a flicker of an eyelash did he act as though anything untoward had happened even though they had come perilously close to the edge—and there was a very deep drop.

'Would it be so very bad if they were married?'

Nell tore her eyes from the *very* deep drop, leaned back in her seat and, holding back her hair from her face with one forearm, looked across at him incredulously.

'*Bad!*' she echoed. 'Bad! Are you mad? Lucy is nineteen, she has her entire life in front of her…a place at university…a career. This is the time in her life when she should be having adventures, discovering who she is, play house if she wants to, but she can't marry some…some…some…' Nell subsided into her seat shaking her head as words and breath failed her at the same moment.

He arched a brow and looked mildly amused by her vehemence. 'Spaniard?'

'I don't care what nationality he is, though the fact he's from the same gene pool as you is no recommendation.'

His grin broadened. 'Felipe does not resemble me.' His young cousin was considered, at least by his overprotective parents, the sensitive soul of the family.

Nell snorted and tossed her head before pressing her nose to the window. She watched the window fog with her breath. After the events of the day—was it really only a day?

She traced her finger across the misted glass before expelling a sigh and leaning back in her seat. She willed her eyes to stay open and tried to fight her way out of the brain-numbing lethargy that was stealing over her. It wasn't the first time—it came in waves.

It wasn't hard to see why sleep deprivation was such an effective interrogation technique.

'Not exactly a big ask.' She struggled to inject a suitable degree of venom into her time-delayed snarling response and was rewarded for her efforts by a laconic grin from Luiz.

'Are we nearly there…?' It wasn't just her anxiety to find Lucy that injected the note of weary desperation into Nell's voice. The longer she remained in this enclosed space with this man, the stronger the urge to escape became.

'If you're a good girl I'll buy you an ice cream when we get there.'

Nell fought off a grin as her eyes drifted to his hands on the steering wheel. He had nice hands—strong, capable hands.

'Perhaps a career and an education are not important to your niece?'

Nell's admiration of his long, shapely fingers came to an abrupt stop. Her wide, indignant eyes flew to his face. 'Lucy is a straight-A student and she has always wanted a career.'

'My cousin is what some people might call a good catch,' he observed mildly.

Nell's hands balled into fists as she glared at him with stormy eyes. 'If you're trying to insinuate that my niece is a gold-digger…' she began in a dangerous voice.

Luiz flashed her a look that was almost pitying. 'I'm trying to suggest your niece might be in love.'

'In *love?*' she echoed, suspecting him of mockery.

'It happens, so I've heard,' he said sardonically.

His dark eyes brushed her face; they were hard and dark. Her lips curled into a derisive smile. He was insulting her intelligence if he thought she was going to buy into the idea of him being a romantic. 'They've only known one another for a few weeks.'

'I take it you're not a believer in love at first sight, Nell?'

Nell rubbed her upper arms briskly—without fail, every time he said her name she broke out in goosebumps. It had to be the sexy foreign accent, she told herself.

She threw back her head and loosed a scornful laugh.

Luiz's attention strayed her way again, his eyes drifting

from her wide dove-grey eyes to her soft quivering mouth. Despite her best efforts to come across as hard-boiled and cynical, Nell Frost just didn't have the equipment.

'I'll take that as a no, shall I, Nell?'

She rolled her eyes and tried to hide the unease she felt at the direction of this conversation. 'I do not. Lust at first sight, possibly.'

'Is this personal experience speaking?'

The sideways flicker of his eyes sent Nell's stomach into a lurching dive. She gave a frozen smile. 'That would be none of your business.'

Imagining he was thinking about he way she had kissed him earlier put an extra layer of defensive ice and scorn in Nell's voice as she added, 'I suppose *you* believe in love at first sight.'

'I have no personal experience of it, but I am not as cynical as you. I would not dismiss it out of hand.'

'The last of the great romantics,' she mocked folding her arms in an unconsciously protective gesture across her chest as she bent her head forward, allowing her hair to fall in a silky concealing curtain around her face. 'So I suppose you think getting married at nineteen is a good idea too?'

'Well, I would be a hypocrite if I rebuked Felipe for something I did myself.'

Nell's jaw dropped as she spun back to face him. '*You* got married at nineteen!' she yelped.

'Twenty actually.'

She shook her head. 'Do I look that gullible?'

His heavy-lidded eyes flashed her way. She looked back at him, her eyes big and wide like a trapped bird. 'Actually, yes, you do.'

'Well, looks can be deceiving,' she retorted.

'Why is it so difficult for you to believe I was married at twenty?'

She looked at him blankly. 'You're serious?'

It was irrational. Why shouldn't he have been married young? But no matter how hard she tried she just couldn't picture him as some starry-eyed, ardent, idealistic youth so in love that he had married his first love despite family opposition—having glimpsed the privileged background he came from, Nell felt the family opposition was a reasonable assumption.

His future had probably been mapped out for him at birth. Unless...the question leapt ready formed to her lips.

'Was she pregnant?' Her groan of horror tacked itself seamlessly onto the sentence. She caught her full lower lip between her teeth and slid a wary look in his direction. 'Sorry, that's none of my business.'

'No,' he agreed flatly, 'it isn't. But for the record shotguns were not required.'

Her brow furrowed as she mused, 'I'd have thought...' She stopped as it occurred to her that she was displaying an un-healthy interest in his personal life.

Besides, with his spooky ability to turn everything around so that she was in the wrong, the fewer words she exchanged with the wretched man, and the least opportunity she gave him to say her name, the better!

She wasn't here to find out what made Luiz Santoro tick—even had she had the inclination, that would in any case take about a zillion years. The man's character had more twists, turns and dead ends than a maze. She was here to find Lucy and extricate her from this situation. The details of *how* she was going to extricate her were a little hazy. But during the drive it had begun to dawn on Nell that something more than logic and reasoned argument might be required.

Just what that *something* might constitute she didn't yet know.

'Thought what?'

She sketched a dismissive smile. 'It doesn't matter.'

'Isn't it a little late to be cautious about sharing your opinion?'

'All right, well, you're not actually the best advertisement for marrying young, are you? I'd have thought considering your marriage flopped, your natural instinct would be to stop your cousin making the same mistake.'

There was a pause while Luiz struggled against his natural instinct to stop the car and kiss her into silence.

An image of a youthful Luiz, all romantic ideals and raging hormones, flashed into her head. She felt a swell of sympathy for the girl he had swept off her feet—and just a tinge of envy?

Nell dismissed the ridiculous thought before it was fully formed and wondered if his ex-wife was devastated when it ended, or relieved. Had she been able to rebuild her life or had she compared every man that came after with Luiz Santoro?

'Did I say my marriage was a mistake?'

'Under the circumstances I took that as read.' Some men could not admit to failure of any sort and he was clearly one of them.

He clicked his tongue. 'You can get into all sorts of trouble that way.'

'Is that some sort of threat?' Nell was appalled to hear a quiver in her voice, so she added with a laugh, 'Am I meant to be scared?' She would have felt a lot happier if it had been fear that was causing her heart to slam against her ribcage.

'If your marriage was such a roaring, screaming success story, how come you got divorced?'

The disdain in her voice caused his nostrils to flare, but there was only mild mockery to read in his voice as he said, 'We did not divorce.'

Brow furrowed, Nell gave a bewildered shake of her head. 'But…?'

There was no discernible expression in Luiz's deep voice as he elaborated. 'We had been married eighteen months when Rosa died.'

Nell, who hadn't thought she could feel more awkward and at a disadvantage in his company, discovered she could. Her hand went to her mouth.

'That's terrible.' Nice understatement, Nell.

He slid her a sideways look; their eyes momentarily connected. 'It was a long time ago.' And all he had left was a memory and it seemed to him sometimes that that too was slipping away from him.

He had stopped grieving for Rosa a long time ago, but he did grieve for the loss of her memory and he felt intense guilt on the days when he closed his eyes and could not see her face, hear her voice or her laughter. They were all slipping away from him. She was slipping away from him.

He turned away from the sympathy in Nell's wide clear eyes. It reminded him of the way people had looked at him in those weeks and months after Rosa had died. Though the sympathy had faded when he had not obliged and fallen apart. His lack of tears and emotion had been viewed with suspicion in many quarters and then when, after what was considered an appropriate period of time, he had not found a suitable replacement for Rosa they had been equally disgruntled.

There could be no replacement for Rosa; a man only loved once.

'Go on, ask me.' He could feel her eyes on his face.

'Ask you?'

At one level Luiz knew that she could not be held accountable for the way her features had imprinted themselves in his mind. On another, more irrational level it felt as though she was usurping Rosa's place in his thoughts.

Nell winced, but did not comment as Luiz crunched the gears. His face in profile looked impassive; she could see a muscle in his lean cheek clench spasmodically.

'You are clearly dying of curiosity.'

'You overrate my interest in your personal life.' She almost immediately contradicted her claim by adding, 'Rosa is a beautiful name—was she?'

'Yes, very beautiful,' he cut across her in a harsh voice.

Of course she was. Nell experienced a spasm of sympathy for the woman he eventually did marry. It would be tough for that woman to know she was being compared to the memory of his tragic lost love.

How could you compete with a ghost?

'Any other things I should know?' She stopped abruptly, her wide eyes flying to his face. 'Do you have any children?' As she spoke an image flashed into Nell's head of Luiz, his dark hair attractively mussed, playing rough-and-tumble games with a dark-eyed boy. Or maybe he had a little girl who reminded him of her mother?

Luiz's jaw tightened as she stared bleakly ahead. When Rosa had wanted children he had refused, saying there would be plenty of time, only there hadn't been. And now there never would be children. How could he have with another woman what he had denied the only woman he had ever loved?

'No children.'

An awkward pause followed his flat rebuttal.

'But do you have a serious relationship…I'm not being nosy—'

'No?'

His sardonic tone made her flush. 'No, I'm not. I'd just like fair warning if there's a jealous girlfriend somewhere who's likely to appear wanting to scratch my eyes out.'

'I do not encourage jealousy.' He was no monk, he had physical appetites, but separating out emotion from sex eased his guilt.

She gave a dry little laugh. For a sophisticated man that was an incredibly naïve comment. 'Looking like you do, you don't need to *encourage* it.' Nell closed her eyes and bit her imprudent tongue; the censor area of her brain appeared to have shut down.

'Thank you, Nell.'

'No need to thank me. It wasn't a compliment, just a statement of fact, and it can't be news. You must know you're drop-dead—good-looking.' Her hasty amendment drew an amused rumble of laughter from him. 'Though,' she added, gritting her teeth, 'just for the record, my personal taste doesn't run to mean, moody and macho.'

'I must take exception. I am considered by some to have a very even, sunny temperament,' he said straight-faced.

Nell fought off a smile and grunted. 'At least you have a sense of humour. That's something.'

'You can relax. There is no one likely to appear with a prior claim—I'm all yours.'

Nell's treacherous stomach flipped. 'Aren't I the lucky one?'

As she absently touched the ring on her finger and thought about the woman who might one day wear it for real she experienced a confusing rush of tangled emotions.

'Your wife—she must have had very slim fingers.'

His jaw tautened. People never mentioned her name in his presence and now she was the main topic of conversation. 'Rosa never wore that ring.'

'Of course not,' Nell muttered, feeling stupid. Obviously he would never taint the memory of his lost love by allowing another woman to wear it.

'She did not care for antique jewellery,' he said shortly.

Nell's eyes widened. 'Oh!' Her glance moved over the pink rose diamond surrounded by rubics—some reject! 'Is this very old?'

'It's been in the family a long time. My grandmother's twin sister Domenica was the last family member to wear it. Her fiancé was British.'

'Really!' It must be marvellous to have a family history that stretched back generations. 'Did they move to England?' she asked, wondering about the woman who had once worn this ring for real.

Luiz shook his head. 'No, her fiancé was killed in World War Two and she remained single.'

Like you, Nell thought. She looked down at the ring, a wave of sadness lapping over her. 'That's so sad!' she said gruffly.

'Are you crying?'

He sounded astonished and no wonder—no doubt he thought it was ludicrous to be so affected by a tragedy that occurred so long ago. She sniffed and lifted her chin.

'No, of course not!' she denied stoutly.

'You just have something in your eye.'

'Funny man. I'm laughing on the inside,' she promised him. 'Why don't you just keep your eyes on the road?'

Yes, why don't you, Luiz? seconded the voice in his head.

CHAPTER SEVEN

LUIZ drove on expecting the car to stop at any minute. In the periphery of his vision he was conscious of Nell's head lolling forward like a rag doll every few minutes, the intervals between her snapping upright getting longer and longer.

'Go to sleep if you're tired.'

She scrubbed a hand across her gritty eyes and yawned. 'I'm not tired.'

The blatant lie drew a heavy sigh from his lips, but before he could dispute her claim the engine faded and they glided to a standstill.

'I wish I could say the same.' Still, it could have been worse. He studied the area. The spot, sheltered from the road by a copse of the almond and oak trees that bordered the slopes, was not too exposed.

'Why have we stopped?' She passed a hand across her eyes and stifled a yawn. She felt stiff and uncomfortable. Her cheek, where it had been pressed into the window, probably looked as creased as her clothes—which were pretty creased.

Beside her Luiz looked as though he'd just stepped out of the shower, except of course his hair was dry and he had clothes on—clothes that looked freshly pressed—and he oozed an indecent amount of vitality for someone who had been driving on hair-raising roads.

She was scowling at the total unfairness of it all and when he turned his head she ignored his smile, lifting her brows in enquiry. 'So why?'

'I wanted to admire the view.'

Nell narrowed her eyes and looked daggers at him.

Luiz gave another smile, this time sardonic as he held up his hands in mock surrender. 'Why do you think we've stopped?'

'If I knew I wouldn't have asked…' She stopped, a look of horror stealing across her face. 'Are you trying to say we've broken down?'

'We have.'

Luiz watched as she dropped her head into her hands and groaned. 'Why do these things keep happening to me?'

'Is that a rhetorical question?'

She lifted her head and glared at him with loathing. 'This is not a good time to be funny. Just in case nobody has mentioned it, you're not good at it.' She took a deep breath and said to herself, 'Don't panic.' She closed her eyes. Stay calm, she told herself. It was probably something simple and they'd be on their way in no time.

'I'll try.'

Nell didn't deign to respond to this open provocation. 'I suppose you know nothing about engines?'

'I'm not an expert but I get by.'

'Good. Then…' she waved in the direction of the car bonnet '…shouldn't you be looking for loose leads or broken fan belts or something?' She had a vague recollection of a pair of tights being used with miraculous effect to repair a broken-down engine on a TV programme—she had no tights but clearly the situation was not hopeless.

'There's no point.'

This defeatist attitude earned him a disapproving frown.

'I already know what's wrong.'

Nell brightened. 'Why didn't you say so?' Silly question—

he obviously got a sadistic kick from seeing her squirm. 'Well, anyway, that's marvellous!' Her smile faded as she studied his face. 'Not marvelous. It's something major?'

'Not major.'

'Well, what?' Nell wanted to shake the answer out of him.

'We've run out of petrol.'

She flashed him an impatient look. 'No, seriously.'

'*Seriously* we have run out of petrol.'

The colour seeped from Nell's cheeks as she stared at him transfixed in horror. The silence stretched. 'Tell me this is a sick joke.'

'No joke,' he said, unbuckling his seat belt. Nell shivered as the evening air sent the temperature inside down several degrees.

'What are you doing?' she demanded, her voice rising several quivering decibels as he calmly stepped out of the vehicle and stretched to straighten the kinks in his spine. 'Ring someone.'

Luiz ducked his head back inside. 'I'm going to stretch my legs, check out the lay of the land and attend to a call of nature. I suggest you do the same before it gets dark. There is no signal here, so no phone.'

Nell glanced nervously out of the window. She was by no means a town girl, but this landscape was bigger than anything she was used to and she didn't even want to think about the remoteness. It was nature at a raw, primitive level that left her senses feeling bruised... With a shudder she turned away.

'*Dark?*' Her glance was claimed and held by Luiz Santoro's mesmeric stare.

She flexed her shoulders as invisible fingers traced a path down her spine. The landscape wasn't the only thing that was raw and primitive around here!

Nell was relieved when Luiz turned his head and lifted his narrowed eyes to the darkening sky. 'I'd say we've got another hour of daylight.'

'Someone might come along,' Nell countered with determined optimism.

'At this time of day?' He arched a sardonic brow. Never a person who avoided reality even when it wasn't pleasant, Luiz saw nothing admirable in Nell's determined blind optimism. 'When did you last see another car?'

Nell swallowed.

As Luiz scanned her face his irritated scowl faded. The air of desperation in her face was not contrived. As his hooded eyes slid to her mouth he was seized by a strong and dangerous desire to kiss that look away to leave in its place the dazed, hazy look of sexual surrender he had seen when he had kissed her earlier.

'Cheer up,' he said, seeing her moist parted lips in his head, hearing her voice begging him to do it again. 'It could be worse.' The lame platitude was a safer alternative, though it still left him with a gnawing ache that didn't feel as if it was going away any time soon.

The sleeping arrangements were going to require some careful thought. Clearly if he didn't want to complicate this already strained situation sharing the back seat was not an option, but it was a temptation.

'Is that a joke? No,' she contradicted flatly. 'For the record it could not…not be worse. *Nothing* could be worse than being trapped in the back of beyond with…' she paused, sucked in a breath and finished on a husky note of sheer loathing '…you!'

A smile played around his mobile mouth as he scanned her face and said with an air of disappointment, 'I thought British fortitude came into play in the face of adversity?'

Nell extended her clenched fists in an effort to impress the urgency of the situation on him. 'Lucy needs me!' she yelled.

'Relax.' At that particular moment Lucy's needs were not to be compared with the urgency of his own.

Nell heard his laconic advice and missed the heat in his hooded eyes and the fine lines of tension bracketing his mouth. She gritted her teeth. If he said that once more she was going to hit him, though, she conceded, her glance slipping to the broad contours of his chest and shoulders, it would probably hurt her more than him. He was all hard muscle and bone.

'I am relaxed!' she snarled through grated teeth.

He gave an admiring whistle. 'And you said that without a trace of irony.'

'I will scream without a trace of irony too.' The warning was only part black humour. She was really struggling to stay in control. She had a lump the size of a golf ball in her throat.

'It's a waste of time to stress about things over which you have no control.'

Nell threw up her hands and glared at him. 'It's easy for you to be philosophical when you don't give a damn what happens to your cousin! You wouldn't have lifted a finger to save him from making a mistake that could ruin the rest of his life.' Her lips curled into a contemptuous smile as she observed him with disgust. 'The only thing you care about is money!' she accused wildly. 'I pity you!'

'I pity me too for having to contend with your sanctimonious ranting.'

'Lucy is—'

Luiz, who was heartily sick of hearing the name, cut across her. 'I'm sure Lucy is safely tucked up in bed.'

'With your cousin—great!' she snorted. 'That's a very comforting thought.

'Then don't think about it,' he advised brutally, almost visibly becoming bored with the conversation.

Deep in denial, Nell shook her head firmly from side to side. 'I'm not budging from this car until you take me to Lucy. I *insist* you take me to her.'

'I'm flattered by your faith in my ability but making the internal combustion engine run on fresh air is beyond my capabilities.'

'How can we be out of petrol? Didn't you check? Or do you normally delegate tedious tasks like that to some flunky? My God!' she exclaimed, shaking her head as she looked him up and down in disgust. 'You're obviously totally clueless.'

An expression of stunned shock on his face, Luiz stared at her in silence that was broken a moment later by the sound of his husky laughter. Some of the tension drained away with the sound.

'I have been called many things before but never that,' he admitted, his mobile lips twitching into a wry smile as he added, 'Not to my face at least.'

Nell regarded him with unfriendly eyes. 'I'm so glad to have amused you,' she said frigidly. There was laid-back and then there was obtuse, and in her opinion someone who could find anything to laugh at in this situation definitely fell into the latter category.

'You are right. I should have checked we had a full tank, but by the time I noticed it was empty we were past the point of no return.'

Nell struggled to maintain her frigid expression. The man had apologised and it wasn't as if he had planned for this to happen. She was also uneasily aware that her own reaction to their dilemma had been slightly excessive. He couldn't be any happier about this than she was.

'Oh, well,' she began flashing a half-smile without looking directly at him. 'I suppose even you are not—' She stopped, a frown forming between her brows as her gaze focused on his lean features. 'By the time you realised…?' Her half-smile guttered. 'You mean you've known for miles that we were going to be stranded?'

'You make it sound as though I had some grand plan.'

'You said nothing!' Nell was outraged at being kept in the dark. God, the man had been totally condescending from the moment they had met, he was calculating and controlling, and the worst part was she'd been allowing him to manipulate her!

Her eyes narrowed—well, no more!

'Hindsight is a great thing, of course. If I'd known I could have been enjoying your hysterical response for the past five miles...'

He flashed a smile of world-class insincerity, but before Nell had an opportunity to respond to his sarcasm he withdrew his head and strolled away into the tall trees. A moment later the dark, sinister shadows in the dense greenery had swallowed him up.

'I'm not getting out of this car!' she yelled defiantly out of the window before adding a plaintive, 'You can't leave me here like this!'

But he could and he had.

Nell, her face set in lines of mutiny, sat there, her back stiff with outrage. This was a nightmare. It couldn't be happening.

She lasted ten minutes before, unable to withstand her inner restlessness, she decided that she might as well take a look around. Force of habit made her remove the keys he had left in the ignition, lock the car and drop them in her shoulder bag before she left the car and traced the path she had seen him take along the edge of a stream and into the copse of tall trees. She had gone a few feet when the ground began to slope steeply.

The incline was hard to negotiate and after a couple of graceless trips she kept her eyes trained on the ground. She didn't see Luiz until she was literally feet away.

'So you decided to join me.'

'I...' She stopped. Luiz was kneeling on the leaf-covered ground fanning a smouldering pile of what looked like leaves and twigs. 'What are you doing?' The tables were turned. For once she was looking down on him. She decided to enjoy the moment of physical superiority while it lasted.

It didn't last. It didn't even start as she studied his face turned half in profile to her and without warning she started to tremble—nothing that showed on the outside but inwardly at her core.

It reminded her of the feeling she'd experienced once when she'd been caught in the middle of a flat open field during an electric storm and had stood helpless to prevent it as the lightning had struck the ground almost at her feet.

The shadows across his face highlighted the purity and strength of his carved features, but it wasn't the aesthetic quality of his male beauty that affected her, but the more raw, earthy aspect that was an integral part of this man.

'I'm building a fire. It will get cold later.'

Nell plucked fretfully at the neck of her shirt. She could have done with some of that cool right now—her overheated skin prickled with heat even though she was shaking with cold.

'What are you—a Boy Scout?' The image that formed in her mind was more of a grown-up version and it wasn't much of a stretch to see him all hunter gatherer, in commando-style camouflage, maybe a hunting knife in his belt.

Her imagination, Nell decided, giving her head a firm shake to clear the image, needed some serious attention! Women had fought for years for equality and what was she doing with her freedom? In sisterly solidarity she was fanta-sising about a caveman!

Her glance slid of its own volition to the spot where a button midway down his shirt had parted to reveal a glimpse of the sort of chest that no Boy Scout could boast. Not unless the modern Boy Scout was endowed with a precocious degree of muscular development and a sprinkling of dark body hair.

Heart thudding hard, Nell dragged her eyes clear and in the process collided with the dark gleam of Luiz's glittering heavy-lidded stare.

Emotion welled in her throat as the air between them seemed to thicken. Nell's stomach muscles, already quivering frantically, clenched viciously. She exhaled hard twice and swallowed as she struggled to escape the sexual thrall that made her limbs heavy and her brain unco-operative.

Continuing to balance lightly on his heels, he prodded the smouldering flames with a stick, igniting a flame. 'I never was a Scout, nor actually,' he conceded, 'much of a team player.'

'Some people might consider that a weakness.' Nell gave her spiky observation even though she didn't imagine for one second that he cared a jot for the opinion of others. His brand of self-sufficiency bordered on arrogance... Actually, she corrected mentally, there was no bordered about it—he was the most arrogant man she had ever met.

He brushed a hand along his jaw that was already showing a visible shadow of dark stubble. 'It was,' he admitted, flashing a grin, 'something that was touched upon in several of my school reports. That and my problem with authority figures.'

'So your schooldays were not the best of your life.'

'Thank you for your concern, *querida,* but I have for the most part overcome my childhood traumas.'

'I wasn't concerned,' she countered, studiously ignoring the mental image in her head of the lonely, misunderstood little boy with the rebellious streak. 'I reserve my sympathy for your teachers, if you were half as annoying then as you are now.'

His low rumbling chuckle was uncomfortably sexy.

'It is true that the English public school system and I were not a marriage made in heaven.'

Her eyes widening, Nell put out a hand to steady herself

as she leaned against a nearby boulder closer to the fire. 'You went to school in England?'

'It's a family tradition.'

'So your cousin went there too.'

Luiz shook his head. 'No, my uncle is in the diplomatic service. He was based in the States for many years. Felipe was educated there.' He turned away from her to throw another log on the fire and sparks flew into the air. As a billow of woody smoke blew into her eyes Nell coughed.

'What do you expect standing downwind? Come over here.'

The scent that made his nostrils flare was more subtle than smoke—the light warm female flowery scent of her body. Somehow his olfactory senses isolated it from the more pungent scents of acrid smoke, warm soil, wet leaves and green growing things.

Luiz's lashes brushed his razor-sharp cheekbones, highlighted by a dull flush as his glittering obsidian gaze slid over the pale oval of her delicately featured face and downwards over her slim body and smooth, slender limbs. She made him think of a bright fragile flower blooming in a dark corner.

Did her skin feel as soft and silky as it looked?

Why was he looking? Why was he wanting—*Dios*, but *want* was a weak, watery term for what he was feeling—to do more than look?

Relax, Luiz, he urged himself, clenching his jaw as he forced air into his lungs through flared nostrils. It was not exactly one of life's mysteries. This was lust, nothing more complex than a chemical reaction—a strong reaction.

Luiz liked to keep his sex life, like the rest of his life, simple and uncluttered. It did not involve internal debates on the texture of a woman's skin. He laid his cards on the table, no forced sentiment or misunderstandings.

He enjoyed relationships with women who had a male

attitude to sex. Women could be as logical as men, but this woman was a stranger to logic.

He knew that liking and common ground were not prerequisites for sexual attraction, or even great sex—but in his experience without them the aftermath, when passion was spent, could become awkward and sometimes even acrimonious.

Not that he was even considering… His glance strayed to the suggestion of a firm cleavage hinted at by the modest neckline of the simple dress and he felt his temperature rise… All right, he was considering, but only hypothetically.

Nell wiped her watering eyes and made no attempt to follow his suggestion. 'Next you'll be asking me to make a bow and arrow and kill small furry things.' The discordant sound of her own shrill laugh drew a wince from Nell, but to her immense relief broke the scary spell that had been growing in the air between them.

She planted her hands on her hips, unwittingly drawing his attention to her feminine outline, and adopted an air of defiance, feeling relieved to realise that the moment had been a by-product of an overactive imagination and exhaustion. Sure, he was a sexually attractive man, if you went for the dark brooding thing, and he could kiss, but, heavens, she didn't even like him!

'Are you going to make us clothes from their skins? Or spear fish…?' The sarcastic remark reminded Nell of how hungry she was.

Luiz looked amused rather than offended by her snarly rant. 'I take it the back-to-nature thing does not appeal to you,' he observed, feeding the first flickering orange tongue of fire with another piece of wood. 'And there are not just cute furry things in these woods. We have wild boar. They can be dangerous.'

Nell glanced nervously over her shoulder. 'Wild boar!' Was he joking?

'Some *estancias* rear them commercially. Ours are wild.'

'We're still on your grandmother's estate?'

He nodded. 'For most of the time we have been driving across area owned by the family.'

Nell was startled. It had to be vast. No wonder he was willing to go to such extreme lengths to inherit.

He looked at her, a teasing light in his eyes. 'Not everyone has the chance to be at one with nature.'

Nell, despairing of her fascination with his long fingers, responded harshly. 'I have no intention of getting back to nature with you!' She intercepted the gleam in his eyes and, flushing to the roots of her hair, shook her head. 'You have a vile mind.'

His wicked, husky laughter sent a sensual shiver of sensation through Nell's body.

Luiz rose from his crouching position, brushing debris from the knees of his jeans. 'Are you sure it's my mind you are worried about?'

Nell was glad of the shadows as she felt the heat wash over her skin. 'I've more things to worry about than your irresistibility. My niece…'

'Your niece is an adult,' he cut back unsmilingly.

'Legally perhaps, but in experience…'

'I thought you said she has been travelling around Europe for the past six months?'

'She is only nineteen.'

'What were you doing at nineteen, Nell? If you can remember that far back,' he added mockingly. Standing there, her face bare of any make-up, her hair loose, she looked younger than the niece she had come to save.

His expression grew stern as he filled the silence. 'You were caring for a dependent parent.'

Luiz couldn't even begin to imagine what that had involved, but to his mind it was not what a young woman on the threshold of life should have been doing.

He felt a powerful surge of anger directed at the older sister and brother who had, it seemed to him, behaved with criminal selfishness.

'There is no comparison,' she protested crankily.

'*I'm* not the one who's making the comparison. This isn't history repeating itself, Nell.'

Nell shook her head, a flicker of bafflement clouding her clear eyes. 'I don't know what you're talking about.'

'I think you do.' Nell's eyes slid from his. 'Your niece isn't being forced to put duty ahead of desire. She isn't making a selfless sacrifice.'

His tone suggested he didn't have a high opinion of people who made such sacrifices and as his meaning penetrated an embarrassed flush of annoyance washed over Nell's skin.

'I'm not some sickly saintly martyr, if that's what you're implying.'

'You didn't feel trapped? Hasn't it occurred to you that the entire personal crusade thing isn't about your niece, it's about you? You can't bear the idea of your niece throwing away what was snatched away from you when you were her age.'

Nell looked shocked by the suggestion that genuinely hadn't occurred to her—not until now anyway.

'That is a ridiculous idea.' Nell greeted the idea with scorn, but beneath her cool rebuttal she was uneasy… Wasn't there a thread of truth in it? 'I'm worried about Lucy…'

As he struggled to contain a strong irrational surge of anger at the girl's name Luiz met her head-on aggressive glare with a narrow-eyed look of seething irritation. Why was the woman refusing to recognise the obvious? He couldn't decide if she was too stubborn or stupid… She was definitely infuriating!

'This isn't about Lucy!' he bellowed.

Her adrenaline levels high, Nell was so immersed in the heated verbal exchange that she almost let the comment pass unchallenged. She even opened her mouth to deliver another sally in the vocal battle when her expression froze. 'Yes, it is.'

'When are you going to stop taking on other people's responsibilities and get around to living your own life?' His eyes narrowed as he searched her face. 'Or is that what you're afraid of?' he suggested, flinging another log onto the fire. Glowing sparks rose up wrapped in a swirling smoky cloud.

Nell recoiled, slightly taken aback by the strength of his goading anger. 'Not you, if that's what you think.'

He moderated his tone and he said softly. 'I'm not trying to frighten you.'

She stuck out her chin. 'I'm not frightened.'

Her defiance filled Luiz with a mixture of exasperation and tenderness—the former was, he thought, understandable, the latter totally inexplicable.

'Look, your niece is young and I agree with you—' He ignored her derisive hoot of mock amazement and added. 'I agree that at nineteen she knows nothing much about sensible decisions, but at nineteen you knew too much. Your niece is not you, Nell. She is a wilful, spoilt child.'

Nell, her protective hackles bristling, sprang to Lucy's defence. 'You know nothing about Lucy! How dare you criticise her? She's a lovely girl.'

Luiz lifted his shoulders in a laconic manner and rolled down the sleeves of his shirt, which had been turned back to his elbow revealing an expanse of strong, hair-roughened forearms, before rising to his feet.

He gave a dispassionate shrug and looked down at her. 'There's no point discussing this—you're too close to it to be objective.' The irony of his observation was not lost on Luiz, who was struggling to retain his own objectivity every time he thought of the family who had let this young woman shoulder the responsibility of caring for her father alone.

'Don't you dare patronise me!' she yelled, glaring angrily at his broad back as he turned away. 'Look at me, will you?' she panted, stumbling across the uneven ground towards him, and grabbed his shoulder. 'Don't walk away while I'm talking to you.'

Luiz spun back. As his hypnotic dark stare settled on Nell's face her hand fell away. She rubbed her tingling fingers against her thigh and, lowering her lashes protectively, looked up at him through the protective dark mesh.

Suddenly the idea of him walking away didn't seem so bad.

'I'm listening.'

And I'm shaking, she thought. 'What did you mean by "too close"?'

'Look, whether we like it or not we're stuck here, so try and relax. This is not Las Vegas, there are no twenty-four-hour wedding chapels—if they are planning to tie the knot they are not going to do it tonight. And look on the bright side— they're young. By now they've probably changed their minds. If you want to be useful go gather some dry wood.'

Forced to tilt her head back to meet his eyes, Nell folded her arms across her chest. 'I don't want to be useful.' I want to go home.

Luiz watched her lip quiver and fought the alien urge to pull her into the protective circle of his arms. Once she was there he was pretty sure that less noble instincts would take over.

As his gaze lingered on her soft, quivering mouth a deep shudder passed through his body. He wanted her so badly he could taste it—he wanted to taste her. The image in his head of him parting her lips and plunging into that sweet, soft warmth within was so powerful that he was nailed to the spot and unable to speak.

When he did break the static silence his voice was harsh.

'The list of what I don't want to do is long.' But not as detailed as the list of what he wanted to do... At his side his fingers curled into fists.

Dios, he could not recall being drawn so blindly to a woman this way. He had always felt vaguely scornful of men who were ruled by their libido and now frustration and a constant level of arousal were making it hard for him to concentrate. 'Do you imagine there are not places I would prefer to be and—'

The anger in his voice, the abrupt shift in his mood aroused Nell's combative instincts. Sticking out her chin she cut across him with a bored, 'And people you'd prefer to be with. I get the message. Well, for the record, you're not the person I'd choose to be trapped on a desert island with.'

CHAPTER EIGHT

DESPITE Nell's claim she had to concede that personality-wise he would adapt more easily than most to such a situation.

Luiz Santoro was a man who liked to be challenged physically and intellectually. The air of urbane sophistication and his handmade designer shoes had fooled her at first, but Nell was belatedly realising that, should the situation demand it, Luiz Santoro would shrug off the veneer of civilisation very easily.

Only a total idiot would find his unpredictable combustible nature exciting. Nell pressed a hand to her stomach but the butterflies carried on rioting. It was not a good time to discover she was actually not that bright.

'This is not a desert island.'

'No,' she said, drawing her thin cardigan tight around her body. 'A desert island would be warmer.' After the day's heat she was feeling the temperature drop.

'There are tried and tested ways to keep warm.'

Her wide eyes flew to his face. The dark, predatory gleam in his eyes sent Nell's stomach into a slow spiralling dive and sent a paralysing stab of lust all the way down to her curling toes. The sounds of the forest faded and all she could hear was the thunderous roar of her blood in her ears as, with his eyes locked on her own, Luiz took a step towards her.

Everything inside Nell screamed to meet him halfway. She had actually lifted one foot when from somewhere a whisper of sanity made her hold back.

'No!'

It was possible she hadn't spoken out loud, that the yell was only in her head, because Luiz didn't respond to it.

The awkward moment stretched as she struggled for breath and control.

'What are you building a fire for anyway? Wouldn't it be more sensible to stay in the car?' The words emerged staccato and breathless.

Luiz gave a shrug. 'Are you always sensible, Nell?'

She swallowed. His dark eyes felt as though they were eating her up. A man had never looked at Nell this way before and it excited and scared her in equal measure.

She ran her tongue across the outline of her dry, quivering lips. 'Yes?'

It was a question that she was silently begging him to disprove. A nerve clenched in his lean cheek as Luiz struggled with himself. Knowing she would respond if he touched her made it harder to listen to the voice of reason that told him this would be a mistake—on so many levels a mistake. A mistake because he knew it would be uncomplicated sex, but would she?

'Sleep where you like. I can't make the decision for you, Nell.'

Nell fixed on some point over his shoulder. 'That means I'll have the car to myself.' She turned and blindly ran.

By the time she reached the car Nell was panting as she struggled to catch her breath. It was nothing short of a miracle that she had only slipped once during her flight. She bent forward, brushed the loose earth from her grazed knees and examined the heels of her hands that had saved her from the ignominy of landing face first in the dirt—they were bruised.

She had escaped lightly, she reflected grimly. Bruised

hands and scraped knees—it could have been a lot worse. Her thoughts drifted back to those tense, sexually charged moments when things could have got seriously out of control. With a sigh she leaned her back against the door and closed her eyes as she waited for her heart rate to slow.

Luiz hadn't attempted to stop her or follow her; Nell hadn't expected him to. He had been offering her casual sex, not a lifetime commitment, and no doubt he had just shrugged and said win some lose some—or the equivalent in Spanish—when she had bolted like a scared rabbit.

She groaned at the memory of her retreat. He probably thought she was insane. He might be right. Nell, unable to decide whether wanting to stay or not staying constituted insanity, gave a slightly hysterical laugh.

Nothing had happened, and there was no point agonising over it. It was well known that mental and physical exhaustion made people act totally out of character.

'Sleep, that's what I need,' she told herself as she reached with a shaking hand into her shoulder bag to retrieve the car keys. With the talk of wild boar she froze at a sharp crackling sound in the undergrowth.

She stayed that way, ears straining, for several minutes and when she continued to sift through the contents of her bag she kept her eyes trained on the undergrowth.

She was as fond as anyone of wildlife, but she felt a little uneasy about face-to-face encounters. A car door between her and any nocturnal visitors would make her feel a lot more comfortable.

When the keys remained elusive Nell made a clicking noise of impatience with her tongue and, dropping to her knees, tipped the entire contents onto the grass.

She scanned the objects spread out feeling irritation initially, not concern, when the keys didn't leap straight out at her. Muttering, 'More haste less speed,' she began to return the contents one by one to her bag. It was when their numbers were reduced by half that she felt the first stirring of genuine apprehension.

When all the contents were returned except the pencil torch that she held in a white-knuckled grip the apprehension morphed into full-blown despair.

She dropped her head into her hands and groaned. The thought of spending the night out here alone filled her with utter horror. But what alternative did she have? Crawl back to Luiz?

Nell shook her head from side to side. 'Absolutely not— never!' That simply wasn't an option.

Face set in a frowning mask of determination, she tapped her forehead with her finger… Think, Nell, think.

Brow furrowed in concentration, she mentally retraced her actions. She had definitely put them in the bag, they weren't there now so logically they must be somewhere… Her glance slid to her scratched knees and her glance swerved towards the trees that were now a dark sinister shadow in the fast-fading light. They must have fallen from the bag when she fell over.

She flicked the switch on the pencil torch and gave a hollow laugh as its feeble beam shone out. A needle in a haystack would be child's play compared to finding the keys in there with this. With a snort of disgust she threw it over her shoulder.

A moment later, regretting the gesture, she felt around in the grass for the discarded torch. It wasn't much but it was all she had. When her fingers closed over the torch she gave a sigh of relief and settled back on her heels, brushing the tears of self-pity from her cheeks with an impatient gesture.

'Show a little backbone, Nell!'

This was Spain, not the Antarctic. She was not going to die of hypothermia. There were no wolves…were there? Unable to resist the impulse to glance nervously over her shoulder, she switched on the torch. She even had a light and tomorrow when the sun came up she would go and find the keys before Luiz even knew they were missing.

Having satisfied herself this was a workable plan and telling herself it would all make a good story when she got back home with Lucy she settled herself for the night ahead.

Nell had not allowed for the altitude. Once the last faint rays of sun slid behind the horizon her thin cotton dress didn't offer much protection from the elements, not to mention the wildlife.

Listening to the sounds of the night, Nell sat with her back pressed to the car, her chin propped on her knees as she hugged herself in an effort to retain a little body heat.

Her imagination in overdrive, she flinched at every little sound as the mountain that had seemed wild but beautiful in daylight became sinister and very noisy. She held her nerve until something warm and furry scuttled across her foot.

A scream locked in her throat, her heart banging against her ribs, she leapt to her feet and ran. Once in the trees she headed towards the glow of the campfire.

Luiz lay to one side of the flames, his back turned to her, his breathing steady and slow.

Holding her own breath and keeping one eye on the sleeping Spaniard, she crept silently to the opposite side of the fire and dropped to her knees, then, taking care not to make a sound, she eased herself into a lying position.

'I hope you don't snore.'

Nell started and turned over. Luiz lay on his back one arm curved above his head, looking at her.

'You're asleep,' she heard herself say stupidly.

'I was,' he agreed. 'But your perfume is very distinctive.'

'I'm not wearing perfume.' Not sure if he had heard her, she raised her voice as she added, 'I changed my mind…about the car. It was stuffy.'

'Ah.'

Nell's relief that he hadn't asked any awkward questions about her change of mind was short-lived. The breath snagged in her throat as he rose to his feet in one fluid motion. Her pulse raced in dizzy, dry-throated anticipation as he walked towards her. At her side he stopped and looked down; his liquid dark eyes made her tremble.

It was when he started to shrug off his jacket that she was able to reassert a little control over her lust-paralysed limbs.

'What are you d…?'

He leaned down and placed his jacket over her. 'Sleep well, *querida.*'

The mortified colour rushed to her cheeks. 'I can't take your jacket.' *The man wants sleep, not you, Nell.*

'And I suppose you are insulted if a man opens a door for you?' he suggested tiredly. Nell, struggling to cope with the intense anticlimax, barely registered the strain in his voice. 'It's late, so allow me one courteous gesture without looking for an insult or ulterior motive.'

After a short strained silence Nell nodded her head and whispered, 'Thank you,' as she pulled the cloth still imprinted with the warmth of his body around her shoulders. 'I am a bit cold.'

He smiled with his eyes—a neat trick and one that never failed to make Nell's insides go mushy. 'The clue was the shivering, *querida.*'

Nell let the casual endearment pass and watched as he walked, tall and effortlessly elegant, back to his side of the fire, pausing to drop a log on the fire on the way.

Despite everything Nell, utterly exhausted, fell asleep almost immediately, though on the point of drifting off she roused herself to ask in a sleepy voice, 'Are there any wolves?'

She didn't hear his reply.

Luiz lay there listening to the sound of her light, even breathing. He did not require a great deal of sleep but when he did he could sleep any place any time—normally. Tonight that ability appeared to have deserted him.

Tonight a lot of things seemed to have deserted him.

Eventually Luiz managed to empty his mind, but he had barely nodded off when the blood-curdling feral sounds of her screams split the night. He leapt to his feet, adrenaline coursing through his veins as he ran to her side, practically running through the glowing embers of the fire on the way.

Dropping to his knees beside her, he laid his hands on her shoulders.

'What is it? What has happened?'

She looked at him blankly with no recognition. He had seen cornered animals look the way she did as she fought wildly to escape.

Luiz made no attempt to avoid the blows of her hands, or subdue her with his superior strength, he just took her face between his hands. 'It's all right...' he soothed, his voice quiet and steady.

Nell's wild, darting eyes meshed with his and gradually her breathing slowed as she relaxed against him, her face pressed into the angle of his chin.

As he cradled her body in his arms he felt her breath warm on his neck, and the tremors that ran through her slender frame at irregular intervals. Luiz stroked her hair gently, filled with a strong need to comfort her.

When Nell finally lifted her head and pulled away a little from him her face was tear-stained and pale from sleep deprivation.

'I'm sorry.' She angled an anguished look of mortification at his face.

'There is no need to be sorry.'

She attempted a smile but it was a weak affair. 'I should

have stayed at the car. I've ruined your shirt.' She loosened her grip on his shirt that now gaped.

'I have more.'

'Ones that have buttons,' she said, smoothing down the fabric with a shaky hand.

He caught her hand and placed it palm flat on the warm skin of his chest. 'It is fine. Are you all right?' He had seen nightmares, had nightmares, but he had never seen such feral, visceral terror before.

Nell couldn't take her eyes off her fingers spread out pale against his dark skin. Her brow puckered, her teeth were chattering hard as she struggled to sound matter-of-fact. 'It was a night terror.'

'Night terror…?'

Nell moved her fingertips slightly and froze, scared but excited, as her fingers skated across his satiny hair-roughened skin. 'I never r…remember…I used to have them when I was a girl. It's more scary for other people than me. I always used to curl up and go back to sleep. I'm sorry if I disturbed you.'

'Disturbed me?' he echoed.

She frowned, puzzling over the strange sardonic inflection in his husky voice as he hooked a finger under her chin and, tilting her face up to his, rasped, 'I wasn't asleep.'

'This has been the oddest day of my life,' Nell confided in a breathless rush.

His expressive lips curled into a sardonic smile. 'It is not over yet. You're not safe back in your library. *Madre de Dios,*' he added, raking her face with a raw intensity that made her tremble, 'I wish you had never left it!'

She flinched at the passionate angry declaration.

'You do know you scared me witless?'

'I scared you?' Nell felt pretty witless herself as he trailed his finger up from her chin and over the curve of her cheek. His actions had all the hallmarks of compulsion as his square fingertip moved across her skin, barely grazing the downy hair on her cheek, his eyes following the track.

It was the tactile equivalent of a whisper but it caused a disproportionate degree of damage to Nell's nervous system. The little shiver of excitement in the pit of her belly expanded and grew into a butterfly tremor of anticipation as the air around them grew dense with sexual tension.

Somewhere above their heads came the eerie predatory sound of a hunting owl.

CHAPTER NINE

THERE was a smoky, unfocused expression in Luiz's dark eyes as he placed one hand behind Nell's head, his splayed fingers sinking deep into her hair as he supported its weight. The bands of colour along the sharp angle of his cheekbones deepened as his eyes moved across the soft contours of her face.

'Yes, you still are scaring me.' He curved his hand around her face and brought his mouth down on hers. The touch was brief, hard and angry.

Nell forced her eyelids open. They felt hot and heavy—as heavy as the strange lethargy that had invaded her limbs. She looked at him and shook her head slowly in a mute plea.

'Don't look at me that way!' he groaned.

He didn't want to feel this way, but there was no element of choice involved. He had been taken over by a force that was stronger than intellect. The feeling this woman awoke in him was primal. It filled every cell of his body, consumed him, and roared in his veins, wiping away his ability to think about anything but sinking into her, possessing her.

He couldn't think around it or past it.

In the glow of the fire she could see the sheen of moisture on the bronzed skin of his face and neck. Her eyes slid lower to where his shirt hung open. His ribcage rose and fell in tune

with his laboured inhalations. She could see the clear delin-
eation of the slabs of ridged muscle on his flat belly.

Things moved deep inside her as emotions she could not
name thickened in her throat—he was beautiful, the essence
of primitive masculinity.

His hand continued its compulsive journey as he angled it
slowly from side to side; the other moved across her ribcage
before tracing a slow path down her spine until it rested in
the small of her back. His fingers were warm through the fine
fabric of her dress.

She felt the tremor that lifted his chest and drew a deep
sibilant sigh from between his clenched teeth.

'You're still cold.'

Nell gave an inarticulate grunt. She didn't feel cold; she
felt strangely disconnected from her body. 'You aren't.' She
could feel the heat from his body—it penetrated the thin
fabric of her dress.

She spread her fingers and trailed them down his chest over
the hair-roughened skin, pushing aside the fabric of his shirt
until she reached his flat belly.

Luiz grabbed her hand and pulled it off his body. *'Madre
de Dios!'* he ejaculated harshly. 'Do you know what you're
doing to me?' he growled as the desire he had held in stern
check all day roared in his veins.

'You're perfect. I just want to touch you.' Nell's eyelids flut-
tered closed as he bent his head and covered her mouth with his.
His lips on hers were warm and firm, the texture, the taste, the
sensory overload drew a whimpery little sigh that was immediately lost in his mouth as he deepened the exploratory pressure.

The kiss ended and, breathing hard like two people who
had just run a marathon, they stared at each other. Nell let her
head flop forward against his chest. Her arms slid around his
middle as she stayed there listening to his heartbeat until he
pulled away, kneeling over her.

As he lowered himself down beside her Nell slid her hands across his shoulders and down the strong curve of his back.

Luiz's dark eyes glittered as he kissed her with a hunger that was both overwhelming and intensely exciting. It was as if he would drain the essence of her. Nell arched her back and looped her arms tight around his neck, opening her mouth to increase the penetration of his tongue. Her fingers tightened into the dark hair on his nape as she felt his hand move under the skirt of her dress.

Luiz lifted his head and looked down into her face, watching her eyes dilate, the pupil swallowing up the cool grey.

When he looked at her the surging swell of primitive possessiveness in his chest expanded. He had never experienced anything this strong when he looked at a woman, never felt this primitive need to claim her as his own.

He heard the breath catch in her throat as he slowly moved his fingers in a series of lazy arabesques along the soft, silky, ultrasensitive skin of her inner thigh. He slid his fingers under the lacy edge of her pants and felt the heat radiating from the moisture at the juncture of her thighs.

'Oh, God, that's…' Nell moaned, her eyelids squeezing closed, her splayed fingers sliding over the satiny skin of his powerful shoulders as the electric tingle spread over her entire body. Her head thrashed from side to side as her nails dug into the skin of his shoulders.

His hands slid under her bottom, pulling her up to him, arranging her knees either side of his thighs as Luiz kissed his way up the exposed curve of her pale throat before claiming her mouth once more.

A dry gasp left her throat as she felt the hard, pulsing impression of his erection grind into the soft flesh of her belly. It was more shocking and more exciting than anything she had ever dreamt; the hot liquid throbbing ache between her thighs intensified to a painful degree.

Nostrils flared, Luiz kissed the damp skin of her neck, breathing in the warm female scent of her before he drew himself up on his knees and pulled away from her, his eyes not leaving hers for a moment as he unfastened the belt of his jeans and kicked them away.

His shirt followed a second later. He was unselfconsciously naked and gloriously—shockingly to her mind—aroused, and the image of his gleaming naked body tightened the hard knot of desire that clutched low in Nell's belly. Her hungry eyes moved greedily over the taut, rippling muscles of his chest and shoulders, then moved lower, skimming the flat, firmly delineated muscles of his belly and lower still.

The greedy glow in her eyes, combined with her awed whisper of, 'You're so beautiful,' raised Luiz's level of arousal several painful notches.

His voice was unrecognisable, his accent thick as he slid into his own language, the liquid words of Spanish spilling from him as he jerked her towards him and, holding her grey doe's eyes in a hot liquid gaze, slid the zip on her dress.

Nell inhaled sharply and lowered her gaze, her lashes fanning across the smooth curve of her flushed cheek as she asked herself what she was doing.

Stupid question. It was blatantly obvious what she was doing, though she struggled even in the privacy of her thoughts to put it in words.

The question was—was it what she wanted?

She almost laughed at the question—wanted? She had never wanted anything so much in her life.

'I want this, Luiz. I want you.'

His long fingers resting lightly on the smooth skin at the base of her spine flexed as the muscle in his lean cheek clenched. *Por Dios,* he was shaking with need; it consumed him from the inside out with the strength of a forest fire.

'And I want you.' Luiz, his voice barely recognisable,

uneven and thickly accented, pulled the dress over her head. Nell shivered as her skin was exposed to the night air.

Heart thudding frantically against her ribcage, she felt his breath against her face as he slipped the catch on her bra and pressed her back onto the mossy surface.

His eyes were deep black pools and Nell felt herself slipping and falling into them, losing herself…wanting to lose herself in him, in all that hard, dark maleness.

Luiz leaned over her, one hand braced on the floor at her side, the other moulding each pink-tipped quivering breast in turn as words of liquid Spanish slipped from his lips.

'I can't bear…' Nell thought she might die from the unbearable sweet, painful intimacy. Her body arched as his lips moved down across her soft belly, while his hands moved lower, sending sweet, sharp shocks of burning sensation through her entire electrified body.

'You're so hot and wet for me,' he purred throatily as he kissed the curve of her neck.

Her thighs parted under the pressure of his knee and he settled himself between them. The touch of his silky hardness as his erection brushed against her thigh drew a primal cry of, *'Please,'* from her parted lips as she struggled to breathe.

He took her hand and, holding her eyes, curled her fingers around his shaft. It was hard as steel, silky and hot.

'That is what you do to me, *querida,'* he slurred thickly before removing her fingers and pinning both her hands over her head.

He slid into her then, sheathing himself deep inside her with one thrust. The shocking sensual invasion drove the breath from her lungs as she struggled for air and cried his name.

Too involved with what was happening to her, the amazing sensation of being filled and stretched, she was only dimly conscious of Luiz's rasping cry of disbelief.

'I hurt…*Madre de Dios,* you…'

Nell bit his shoulder. 'I'm not hurt, I'm…oh, God, please, Luiz, you're…' She felt some of the rigid tension in the muscles of his back loosen as he began to move slowly. She stroked his back, her fingers digging into the sweat-slick smoothness, and clung, wrapping her legs around him as he moved, slowly at first and then, in response to her desperate cries, harder.

He felt the first ripples of her contraction and, losing the tight, painful control, he buried himself deep in her and let go. The climax shattered him and left him gasping for breath as he collapsed onto her.

Nell opened her sleepy eyelids and blinked. As the leafy canopy above her head slid into focus the night's events came rushing back.

'Oh, God!' She sat bolt upright, her wide eyes scanning the clearing.

There was no sign of Luiz. She was alone in the clearing, the smouldering embers evidence of the blazing fire, and the new aches in her body the evidence of the lovemaking.

'Oh, God!' she wailed again.

A one-night stand!

She had always wondered what mind-numbing sex would be like and had secretly feared she was too repressed to ever find out first hand, but she had —now she knew!

The learning curve had been steep, but she'd had a pretty good teacher. An image of Luiz's face flashed into her head.

In her naivety she had always thought that for perfect sex you needed a meeting of minds, of hearts, but last night had disproved this theory totally. She was shocked and in equal measure fascinated by the instincts that had burst into life and taken her over—instincts that had been so dormant she hadn't even suspected they existed, that she was capable of such un-restrained passion.

She ran her tongue across her lips. They still felt swollen and sensitive from his kisses. A thrill ran through her as she touched her mouth, her eyes clouding hazily as moments of the passionate coupling flashed across her vision.

It could have been worse, she told herself—she could have fallen for him.

It had been sheer insanity! But beautiful insanity. Before she could dwell on the details of that depravity she heard the sound of movement in the distance.

Hastily she pushed aside the jacket that was covering her and, dropping to her knees, scrabbled for the clothes that had been hastily discarded the previous night.

She slid her dress over her head, swearing softly when her zip snagged halfway up.

'You're awake.'

Standing there barefoot and poised for flight with her hair tangled, her big eyes wide and wary, she made him think of a woodland nymph.

'You should have woken me. What time is it?' He looked incredible in a sexy, rumpled way; she, on the other hand, must look like a bag lady. The world was not a fair place.

He raised a brow at her querulous tone. 'Not a morning person?'

Nell dragged a hand through her hair and pushed it behind her ears and didn't allow herself to think that he might be seriously interested in finding out. They were two ships that passed in the night, or in this case collided. 'I prefer waking in a bed, curtains, sheets.'

His eyes darkened. 'That could be arranged.'

She flushed, her eyes falling from his. '*My* bed.'

'I have a bed.' And he could see her in it, but she was not mistress material.

Nell angled a direct look at his lean face. 'Is that an invitation, Luiz?' Was that shock in his eyes or just alarm? Neither possibility would have surprised Nell considering the irony she had intended to inject into her words hadn't materialised.

Good question, Luiz responded silently. There was quite clearly only one answer, or there had been until he had returned and found her looking so delicious.

When he had left to organise petrol thirty minutes earlier he had not been thinking about a repeat performance of the previous night—well, he had, but only in a 'this would be a very bad idea' kind of way.

He had made love to a virgin. To his mind that automatically put him in the wrong even though she could, she *should*, have told him. *Dios,* it just wasn't something a man expected, and he was used to women who were as relaxed and open about their sexual needs as men.

If she had told him he wouldn't have—would he?

The question hung there. Could he, hand on heart, swear that if she had told him things would have turned out differently?

The silence stretched as he presumably struggled to come up with a way to let her down gently. Nell decided to do the kind thing and let him off the hook.

'Look, you really don't have to pretend last night was the start of a beautiful friendship.'

Friendship was what he had shared with Rosa, lots of high quality friendship, but had their relationship been lacking a vital spark? The moment the disloyal thought formed Luiz felt a vicious stab of guilt that added a harsh note to his voice as he responded.

'Last night had nothing to do with friendship.' And everything to do with a blind, compulsive lust that even now was making its presence felt.

'Do you reserve that sneer for women who sleep with you on the first date?' Nell struggled to inject a note of amusement into her voice.

Luiz angled an incredulous frown. 'We didn't have a date. You were a virgin.'

'You make it sound like a contagious disease. Well even if it was I'm no longer infected.'

'This is not a joke.'

Nell watched the muscles in his brown throat work. He was angry but she couldn't figure out why exactly.

'There was a farm a mile or so farther up the road. I have petrol, some food and a flask of coffee. The car was locked. I'm assuming you have the keys.'

Nell's eyes widened. Other things—she determinedly pushed away the details that crowded into her head—had taken the key situation right out of her mind.

'Slight problem.'

Luiz raised a dark brow and looked expectant; she swallowed. The dark shadow on his chin gave him a piratical appearance and emphasised the brooding danger that was always just below the surface in him.

'I did lock the car. It's sensible to take precautions,' she added, anticipating his mockery.

What she didn't anticipate was the stern expression of self-recrimination that spread across his face. 'It was unforgivable.'

Nell, taken aback by the vitriolic harshness in his manner, blinked. 'What was? Locking the car?' She stopped as it clicked, a dark tide of colour washing over her skin.

'You mean the sex—I was not exactly unwilling.' The recollection of how *not* unwilling she had been brought a dark crimson flush to Nell's cheeks.

'But you didn't know what you were doing.'

'Thanks a lot.'

The bitter retort drew an impatient frown from him as he caught her meaning. 'Do not be ridiculous. You were—'

He paused and Nell inserted her chirpy tone at variance

with the pain locked in her chest. 'Good, bad or indifferent? Do you always grade your one-night stands?'

'Do not speak of yourself that way and do not cheapen what we shared.' Luiz was shocked that the words had emerged from his own mouth…because he did not share. Sharing was for Rosa.

Unaware of the inner devils he was fighting, Nell looked at him in shock.

'I simply wanted to promise you I do not make a habit of having unprotected sex.' His irresponsibility weighed heavily on Luiz.

'I hadn't really thought about it.' It was one of many things she was trying not to think about, but it wasn't easy when the object of your persistent carnal fantasies was standing there talking about unprotected sex.

The admission did not lighten his mood. If anything his expression grew sterner. 'Well, you should.'

He was right, of course, but his sermonising manner struck her as ever so slightly hypocritical. 'Wasn't it you that advised me not to worry about something I have no control over?' Control was what she ought to have shown the previous night, Nell reflected grimly.

'I want you to know that I am prepared to live with the consequences of my actions.'

'What consequences? Once I have found Lucy we're never going to see one another again.' A little time and distance and she might be able to look on last night with a little more objectivity.

'"What consequences?"' he echoed.

His meaning hit her and the colour rushed to her face. 'Oh!'

Lips compressed into a thin smile, he nodded. 'Exactly. I am not a man who walks away from his responsibilities.'

She stuck out her chin and curled her lips into a smile of mild contempt and turned away from him to cover her acute embarrassment, saying, 'I'm not your responsibility. Statistically the chances of getting pregnant the first time—or even the second—must be minimal. And don't worry—if I'm pregnant you'll be the last to know.'

She hadn't taken a step before a hand on her shoulder swung her back. His fingers closed around her upper arms as he jerked her towards him until their bodies collided.

His dark eyes drilled into her. 'It is not a subject for humour.'

She said. 'Obviously not.' And rubbed her arms where she could still feel the imprint of his fingers.

She assumed that he was scared rigid at the thought of an unwanted pregnancy.

'No more jokes,' she promised. Suddenly she didn't feel much like joking; his reaction was natural, but hurtful all the same.

'I have never had unprotected sex with a woman, not even my wife.' There was a confessional quality to the words that spilled from him. 'Rosa wanted a baby, I said there was time, only there wasn't.'

Nell's tender heart ached to see his pain. 'You couldn't have known.'

Ignoring her sympathetic intervention, Luiz continued as if she hadn't spoken. 'I wouldn't give her the child she wanted and now with you, a woman I barely know…you could be carrying my child.'

His words explained a lot and hurt her on more levels than she knew existed.

'Well, I'm not, so let's just change the subject…the keys.' She snatched a little wildly for her bag that lay on the floor, brushing the inexplicable moisture from her cheeks as she did so. 'They were in here,' she explained, straightening and looping it across her shoulder. 'They must have fallen out when I slipped,' she confessed.

'You lost the keys?' He could not believe he had said

those things to her. What was it about this woman that made him forget a lifetime of keeping his own counsel and guarding his emotions?

It seemed to Nell he was avoiding looking at her, she couldn't read anything in his voice, but he had to be unhappy about the keys. She couldn't allow herself to think about the other things he was unhappy about.

'I didn't do it on purpose—it was an accident.' Would the same excuse work for sleeping with a man you barely knew, and wanting to do it again even though he was not only clearly regretting it like mad, but still in love with his dead wife?

'It was dark,' she added, wishing it were dark now because she felt as though her carnal cravings were written all over her face.

What had happened to pride and self-respect?

'I was going to get up early before you were awake...' Their eyes met and she blushed. 'That was the plan anyway.'

He extended his hand and opened his fingers. The key lay in his palm. 'I thought it might be something like that.'

Nell's eyes lifted from the keys to his face; two circles of colour appeared on her cheeks. 'You had them all along.'

'I found them near the car.'

'But you just thought you'd make me squirm? What a nice man you are.' A flash of something that on anyone else Nell would have interpreted as remorse appeared in his eyes.

'Last night should not have happened.'

A mortified flush climbed up her neck until her face was burning. 'Don't dwell on it. I won't.'

'Because losing your virginity is something that happens every day of the week.'

'It had to happen some time.'

'You are very casual about it.'

'For heaven's sake, will you stop going on about it?' She gave a shrug and tried to inject some humour into the situation. 'Relax. I realise the last time you slept with a virgin you married her, but I'm not expecting a proposal.'

'I have never slept with a virgin before.'

'Oh! I assumed that as you were both so young your wife…' He raised a sardonic brow and Nell broke off mid-sentence, colouring deeply. This was one of those occasions when you had to recognise the hole you had just dug was deep enough.

'Rosa was not a virgin, I was.'

'*You* were a *virgin?*' She struggled to picture a youthful and inexperienced Luiz.

'Young men frequently mature later than girls, though not it seems in your case. Now turn around and let me fasten your dress.'

'I can manage.'

Luiz ignored her. 'Turn around.'

Face set, she did, mainly because it was easier than arguing. 'It's jammed.'

She rolled her eyes at his assessment. 'I could have told you that—' She stopped as his fingers touched the bare skin of her back and gasped as the contact sent a slug of sensation swirling through her body.

'I almost have it. There, done.'

'Thank you,' she muttered, not looking at him. He was much better at taking off clothes.

Nell took some of the coffee he had brought and forced down one of the delicious pastries, if only to delay the moment when she had to get in the damned car beside him.

When he asked if she was ready to leave she took a deep breath and painted on a smile.

'When you are,' she agreed cheerfully.

'Try not to worry about Lucy,' Luiz said as she clicked her seat belt.

'I'm not worried.' That was the problem—until he had mentioned her Nell hadn't thought about Lucy all morning.

CHAPTER TEN

IT only took half an hour to reach the cottage and Nell spent most of that time with her head poked out of the window, but the seething silence in the car made it one of the longest journeys she could recall ever enduring.

Nell flashed an occasional look at Luiz's profile, not out of choice, but because her eyes drifted in that direction of their own volition with worrying frequency. On every occasion he looked remote and aloof.

It was probably better that way. If last night was any gauge a smile might be enough to make her start ripping off his clothes, she thought with a wince of self-disgust. No, a bit of distance was what was needed right now and she could live without his smiles, though it might be nice if he noticed she was alive.

The man had no manners.

The potholed road they were travelling diverged and Luiz took the right fork that led through a pair of open wrought-iron gates.

'We're here?'

'Yes.'

Nell looked around. The building they had pulled up in front of was not a cottage as she understood it. The home she had just sold had been advertised as a large comfortable family home, this cottage was probably four times its size.

Single-storey and stone built in the style of a Mediterranean villa, it had wisteria rather than roses growing around the door.

It was certainly secluded enough for a love nest.

He nodded and said flatly, 'That's it.'

'Well, I just hope they're here after all this.'

Luiz, on whom the significance of the absence of a car had not been lost, thought she might well be disappointed. He kept the opinion to himself as she virtually exploded from the car and ran, skirt hitched above her shapely knees, over the gravel to the front door.

Nell looked around for a bell but could find none so instead banged her fist on the wooden panelling. The door immediately swung inwards and she almost fell inside.

She turned and yelled back to the car. Luiz was still sitting there watching her and she shook her head, impatient with his total lack of urgency.

'It's open!' she yelled, and stepped inside yelling her niece's name.

Luiz took a deep breath before he entered through the front door she had left open. The last time he had been here had been after the funeral. He had vowed on that occasion never to step through the door again; now here he was and very little had changed, except the raw intensity of his pain.

He had expected to feel…what?

Pain? Melancholy? Nostalgia…?

He had expected to feel *more* and coming in the wake of last night's emotional betrayal it only intensified his guilty discomfort.

He had entered the hallway when Nell reappeared with a clatter on the polished wooden floor, breathing hard, her soft features contorted in anxiety and frustration. Her eyes shone with accusatory anger as she levelled a glare at him.

'There's nobody here.' Her voice was hoarse from yelling. 'You said they'd be here!' she accused shrilly. 'And—' this was the worst part '—I believed you.' She couldn't believe she had not even paused to question the possibility he might be wrong.

'I said this was the place they would be most likely to come,' he corrected. 'They were here or somebody was—'

Nell rolled her eyes. 'What are you—psychic?'

'There are fresh car tracks outside in the gravel.'

She gritted her teeth; his calm was totally maddening. 'Which is no help at all. Don't just stand there, do something!'

He raised a laconic brow and she wanted to shake him. 'What would you have me do, Nell?'

Nell regarded him with simmering frustration. 'I thought you always knew what to do.'

His eyes narrowed. 'Where you are concerned,' he observed drily, 'what I do is always the wrong thing.'

Like sleeping with me. 'And you care so much for my opinion!' she snorted.

'I—'

'Luiz! What are you doing here?'

At the sound of his name Luiz turned his head. 'Good morning, Felipe.'

Nell spun around to face the doorway where a young man stood. He was dressed in jeans and a shirt like Luiz; there the similarities ended. The newcomer, who was a little above average height, had a slim, boyish build. He wore horn-rimmed spectacles and had shoulder-length floppy brown hair that gave him an earnest, slightly disheveled student look.

'I was looking for you.'

His cousin looked confused. 'You were? Did we arrange something? I forgot. I thought you didn't come here any more. I didn't go into the studio.'

'It's empty, Felipe.' It had seemed wrong to him to hide away Rosa's talent behind dusty covers; her work was permanently displayed in a gallery in Seville.

'He's Felipe? *You're* Felipe?' Nell, following very little of this interchange was unable to hide her doubt. She looked from one man to the other. Man in the case of the younger Santoro was a stretch; she doubted he had started to shave yet.

Reality and imagination were poles apart and she struggled to reconcile her mental image of a slick seducer of young women with the fresh-faced youth before her.

'This is Felipe. Felipe, this is Nell Frost.'

The boy's eyes widened. 'You're Lucy's Aunt Nell!' he exclaimed.

Nell took a step towards him feeling suddenly rather old. 'Yes, I'm Lucy's Aunt Nell. Now where,' she demanded sternly, 'is Lucy?'

He shook his head. 'I d-don't know.'

The faltering response did not impress Nell, who waved a warning finger in his direction. 'Please do not muck me around—my patience is not infinite.'

'Her patience is non-existent.'

The sly aside drew a repressive glare from Nell. 'Do you mind? I'm talking to your cousin. Now, Felipe, what have you done with Lucy?'

'I haven't done anything with her. She…I don't know…I tell you I don't know. She took the car last night and left me here. She said she was going home. I don't understand—she said she loved me and now, now says she is not ready for marriage and…' The boy's voice broke as he buried his face in his hands.

Nell expelled a gusty sigh and breathed a fervent, 'Thank God!' A loud sob brought a guilty grimace to her face.

'I love her!' Felipe, the picture of heartbroken misery, wailed.

Nell's tender heart was touched by his anguish, but her sympathy was tinged with a touch of shame. It probably made her guilty of a variety of sexism, but she didn't have a clue how to cope with a man who was crying.

She glanced towards Luiz, who was a man, but not one, she was guessing, who had much personal experience of public displays of any form of weakness. But despite that she'd seen his vulnerability—did he resent that?

She caught his eye and mouthed, Do something, but he shrugged and continued to look at his cousin with mild distaste mingled with not so mild irritation.

The man seemed to have no heart, but she knew he had— had he wept when his wife died?

Nell pushed away the thought, because feeling any form of empathy with Luiz Santoro could, she instinctively knew, take her back into a dangerous place. She brushed past him and gave a loud contemptuous sniff. Her voice soft with sympathy, she smiled encouragingly at Felipe.

'Of course you love her,' she soothed, feeling disloyal but unable to repress the horrified thought that Lucy might be the sort of girl that mothers warned their sons about.

Watching his shoulders heave as he struggled to control himself, Nell placed a tentative hand on the shoulder of the distraught young man. 'There, there,' she said awkwardly.

The effect of her sympathy was to make tears spring to his eyes.

'Enough, Felipe!' Luiz's tone, brusque bordering on brutal, appeared to be effective—his cousin's lips stopped quivering and he listened as Luiz continued speaking to him in Spanish.

He responded in the same language before turning to Nell and saying softly, 'I am very sorry, Miss Frost, for causing you so much worry.' He turned to Luiz, who gave an almost imperceptible nod.

Nell rounded on Luiz. 'Did you tell him to say that to me?' she asked in a dangerous voice. 'Dear God!'

'If I did?'

'The poor boy is not a puppet!' She turned back to Felipe, who looked a little startled by her fierce instruction to, 'Ignore *him* and tell me what happened.'

'We were in love…'

Nell shook her head and said sharply, 'No, not that bit.'

Felipe shook his head in a confused way and looked ready to bolt or burst into tears again.

Nell felt a surge of frustration and impatience and opened her mouth to tell him to pull himself together until she realised with horror that she was behaving as heartlessly as Luiz.

She forced herself to smile. 'Why are you here alone, Felipe? Did you have a row? When did Lucy leave?'

'She thinks you had a row and buried the girlfriend in the garden.'

Nell responded to the sardonic interruption with a gritted, 'Will you be quiet? Or I'll bury you in the garden.'

Luiz met her fulminating glare with a look of patently insincere innocence that drew a low growl from Nell's throat. 'You're totally impossible.'

A wide grin of the painfully attractive variety spread across Luiz's face as he inclined his dark head in acknowledgement as the tension between them perceptively thawed. 'Thank you.'

Nell caught herself grinning back and instead compressed her lips into a thin line. 'That was not a compliment,' she said repressively.

Felipe, who had been visibly struggling to follow the quick-fire interchange, shook his head. 'I would never hurt Lucy.'

'Of course you wouldn't, Felipe.'

'She left this morning some time…I think…'

Nell, unable to contain her impatience, cut across him. She

just prayed that her niece had not got into more trouble. 'You *think*—you don't *know?*'

'Not really. She left while I was asleep.' He wiped a hand across his damp face and pulled a crumpled sheet of paper from his pocket. 'She left me a note and took the car. I was stuck—'

Luiz interrupted. 'What about your phone?' His glance slid to Nell and he added in a low-voiced aside, 'There is reception here.'

'It was in the car when Lucy left.'

'She stranded you here?' Nell exclaimed, appalled.

'Your niece sounds like a very...resourceful young woman, *querida*.'

Nell cast him a look of seething dislike. 'Do not call me that—I'm sure Lucy didn't mean to strand you.'

Felipe looked shocked by the suggestion. 'Oh, no, not Lucy.' Nell lowered her eyes. Clearly his cousin had all the cynicism in the family. 'She said in the note that she'll always treasure our time together. This wasn't just a holiday romance.'

Nell had some sympathy for Luiz's grimace, but she hid it, and when he delivered the pithy advice to Felipe to get a grip on himself, before adding something in rapid Spanish that she was guessing from his cousin's expression was not flattering or sympathetic, she narrowed her dove-grey eyes and flashed him a warning look.

'You are not helping.' She turned with a smile to the younger Santoro. 'Did Lucy say where she was going? I'm sure she was very upset. She might need—'

'You?' Luiz inserted. He gave a laugh. 'I don't think so, *querida*. Accept it—your niece is a young woman who is well able to take care of herself.' His dark gaze moved across the soft contours of her face. More so than her aunt, it seemed to him.

'She'll be at the airport by now.'

Nell dragged her attention from Luiz and turned back to his cousin. 'Airport?'

Felipe nodded. 'She put the flight details in the letter.'

'What a romantic letter,' Luiz drawled

Nell gritted her teeth. 'So help me if you say one more word.' She turned back to Felipe, who was looking startled to hear the cousin he was more than a little in awe of addressed this way.

'Lucy said if she didn't catch this flight she'd miss…' he consulted the crumpled sheet of paper '…freshers' week? If you'll excuse me I'll just…' With a vague smile he vanished through the door, closing it carefully behind him.

Nell folded her arms across her chest, unwittingly pushing her breasts upwards to reveal the suggestion of a cleavage. It was not a suggestion that Luiz was unaware of.

'So you are happy now? It would seem that your niece is not the hopeless romantic you thought, but a pragmatist.'

Nell, who was aware that Lucy did not emerge from this all that well, elevated her chin to a defensive angle. 'I suppose you think she's behaved badly.'

'I have not thought about it. The truth is I have no particular interest in your niece—she was a means to an end.' The end had not been intended to include a total breakdown in self-control or the most erotic, mind-blowing experience of his entire life.

Nell's eyes dropped to the ring on her finger. God knew how but somewhere along the way—possibly when she had lain beneath him and begged him to take her—she had lost track of why Luiz was here. He was holding up his end of the bargain.

Of course, she had given a lot more than their contract demanded.

'You'll have your money, so you're not bothered. I don't suppose you even care that your cousin is heartbroken.'

The ease with which she believed the worst of him brought a steely glint to Luiz's eyes. 'Ah, yes, I have my money.'

The peculiar inflection in his voice made her ask again. 'Don't you?'

'As for Felipe,' he said, well aware that he had given Nell

Frost little reason to think the best of him, 'I'd like to think he has learned something from the experience but I doubt it.'

'God, you are so callous!' Nell exclaimed in disgust as her glance swerved towards the door the jilted young man had walked through.

'And you are so inconsistent. We are speaking of the person you have spent the last twenty-four hours cursing and now—' Luiz shook his head. It had always baffled him how women were drawn to needy men who needed mothering. 'Now,' he drawled, feeling a strong repugnance for the accompanying image that flashed into his head of his young cousin enjoying Nell's embrace and maybe even returning it, 'you wish to kiss him better.'

As if they were attached to a string Nell's eyes were drawn to the sternly sensual outline of Luiz's mouth. She swallowed and, losing her concentration, allowed her thoughts to drift to a place where his body was hot, heavy and hard on top of her. A place where his tongue made erotic, stabbing incursions into her mouth.

For long moments Nell forgot to breathe. And only remembered she needed to when the sexual fog that clouded her brain began to lift. Struggling frantically to draw air into her tight chest, she made the fatal mistake of allowing her eyes to connect again with Luiz's.

His smoky stare was as dark as the feelings that broke free inside her when she looked at him and thought about touching him—the two were impossibly linked in her head.

Low in her pelvis things twisted hard, drawing a little gasp from her parted lips as she fought the enervating languor that nailed her to the spot. Heart thudding, she felt the heat rush to her cheeks—she might as well put up a sign, she thought in exasperated dismay: yours for the taking.

For a moment she thought he might be about to take up the invitation.

He took a step forward, then jerkily, without his normal fluid grace, stepped back and looked down at her with all trace of emotion wiped clean off his face. She might have believed the moment had all been a construct of her overheated imagination had it not been for the muscle that clenched and unclenched like a time bomb in his cheek.

'I do not go in for indiscriminate kissing.'

'Imagine how privileged I feel.'

Nell ignored the nasty interjection. 'Now I've seen Felipe I realise that he is—'

'Pathetic?'

The suggestion drew her wrathful glare. 'Did you have to speak to him that way?'

'Yes,' Luiz said bluntly. 'I have no objection to Felipe suffering. I'm sure it is character-forming.' In his opinion his cousin could do with some. He made allowances because he had a fiercely protective mother; however, there were limits. 'But I would prefer he did so in silence.'

'Because real men don't cry?' Nell shook her head and directed a look of contemptuous disbelief at him. 'They should be strong and silent much like yourself, possibly. God, I pity your son if you ever have one.' With each successive accusation her temper rose and Luiz's seemed to cool in a corresponding degree. By the time she flung a shrill, 'You have the sensitivity of a brick!' his face looked as though it were carved in stone.

Nell met his dark gaze and realised with a sudden flash of piercing insight that she wasn't angry with him because he didn't appear to care about his cousin, but because he didn't care about her!

Her eyes widened, then as the implications of her discovery took hold her lashes swept downwards across the curve of her marble-pale cheeks.

God knew she had no right to expect anything from him.

She had no right to expect him to care—she didn't care. Last night had not been about caring; it had been a moment of insanity. She had told herself, she had not *stopped* telling herself, that last night had been a one-off, but still in a secret unacknowledged corner of her heart she wanted more.

'I have—'

Her lashes lifted as he began to speak and Luiz stopped dead—the wide, luminous dove-grey eyes that met his were shimmering with unshed tears. His anger fell away in a rush and tenderness that took him totally unawares rushed in to fill the vacuum.

Shock at the intensity of his feelings made Luiz's voice harsh as he caught her arm and urged her into a chair. 'Sit down before you fall down.'

Nell, struggling to summon some defiance in the face of his obvious irritation, shrugged off the hand that lay heavily on her shoulder.

'Will you stop telling me what to do?'

His jaw tightened. 'What's wrong?'

Nell looked at him and thought, I want something from you…something *more*… She passed a hand across her face. She had no intention of voicing her thoughts—she had lost her mind, but not to that extent. She didn't have a clue what the *more* she craved from him was, and even if she had been able to put a name to it she didn't have the right to ask.

'Nothing.' The point was, even having her somewhat limited social life, she hadn't been a virgin at twenty-plus from lack of opportunity, but from choice.

She just wasn't equipped for the entire sex-without-emotional-involvement thing. She didn't think she was strait-laced or prudish. A healthy sex drive was nothing to be ashamed of; she just didn't have one—or so she had thought!

Nell's glance slid of its own volition to the sensual outline of Luiz's mouth. She swallowed and pressed her hand to her chest to contain the flutter that climbed into her throat as erotic images crowded into her head.

Clearly Luiz had what she lacked: an ability to separate his sexual needs from his emotional ones. He wasn't going to be experiencing this awful, aching, empty feeling—it was good old-fashioned and utterly illogical guilt. She inhaled deeply, causing the bodice of her dress to chafe against her oversensitive breasts. It could be worse—she could have fallen for him!

The laugh that left her aching throat just stopped short of hysteria—*just*. No wonder he was looking at her as though she were a freak; in his world twenty-five-year-old virgins were probably about as freaky as it got.

'Stop looking at me like that,' she snapped.

Luiz, who only ever dated women who smiled at him and told him he was wonderful, found himself for some bizarre reason not disliking her cranky manner—it was probably the novelty value.

She had more prickles than a porcupine. A slightly unfocused expression drifted into his dark eyes—she had not felt prickly in his arms. She had felt soft and supple, responding to his touch without reservation—she had given without expecting anything in return, given without reservation. A need to feel her softness again right now and here of all places, Rosa's place, swept through him until every cell in his body ached with it and he felt shame at his weakness.

'Like what?'

'You try and be aggravating,' she accused.

He didn't deny it and carried on looking.

'*What?*' she said, feeling totally unnerved by his scrutiny—actually, not totally. That came when he answered her.

'The sex, it was good.' His narrowed gaze slid to her mouth, he swallowed and admitted in a throaty purr, 'Better than good.' He added something in Spanish that sounded throaty and sexy and probably indecent so she was glad she didn't understand him.

'I've not an awful lot to compare it with, but it was not something I will forget in a hurry.'

'I have a lot to compare it with—'

'Please spare me the details, I have a sensitive stomach,' she begged, not joking.

'What are you doing?' he asked, watching her tug at the ring on her finger.

'What does it look like? I'm trying to get this damned thing off—'

'I will not forget it either.'

Nell's head came up with a jerk. Cheeks tinged with pink, she regarded him warily.

'I suppose you're wondering why I slept with you? I've been thinking about it.'

'So have I.'

His deep voice made her stomach flip, but Nell determinedly ignored it and she pushed aside the erotic images of intertwined sweaty limbs that his husky comment had triggered. She opened her mouth to say sorry and stopped herself—why should she apologise? He ought to take at least fifty per cent of the blame.

'No!' She held up her hand, shook her head and, just to get her point over, said it again. 'No!'

'You introduced the subject,' he said mildly.

Nell raised her narrowed eyes to his. 'If I had set out to seduce you I would say sorry. If I deliberately misled you in some way I would say sorry, but I didn't do either and I'm not going to apologise,' she added fiercely, 'for a moment of utter madness.' She started to rise, found her legs were shaky and sat back down again.

'You regret what happened?' Regret—what was to regret?

He silently answered his own question—oh, if you didn't count losing your virginity to a man you barely knew on the floor in the middle of a damn wood…no soft music, no gentle seduction, just a raw, unpolished explosion of hunger. Shame was a sour taste in his mouth.

She had tasted sweet.

At the time the significance of her little gasps of shock had not hit him; they had not made him hold back and make allowances for her inexperience; they had only aroused him more.

The one time in his life he had lost control in the bedroom, and it hadn't been the bedroom and she had been… His mouth curled into a grimace of bitter self-reproach. *Dios,* it was a wonder, he told himself, that Nell had not run screaming for the hills.

But she had not.

She had responded to him with a sweetly wild, unrestrained passion that had been equal to his own, as if the same fire that had heated his blood and wiped all sane thought from his brain had also pumped through her veins.

His eyes darkened and he was helpless to control the response of his body as he savoured the sweet memory of her deliciously wild, abandoned responses to his lovemaking.

A woman could lose herself in his eyes, she thought, mesmerised by the glow in his fixed black stare. She took a breath and pulled her eyes clear.

'When they reach a scary point in their lives some people bury themselves in their work to avoid dealing with it,' she continued, her voice gaining confidence as she spoke—this was a subject she had given some thought to on the journey, thought, *not* rationalisation.

'Me—' Nell pressed a hand to her chest and gave him a lopsided grin, hoping she was coming across as someone who had dealt with this and come out the other side able to be objective, able to see the funny side.

What funny side?

'I jumped on a plane for what turned out to be no good reason, then I jumped into bed with you—well, not bed, but you know what I mean. I was…actually I'm not sure what the psychological term is for what I did, or if there is one—'

'Oh, I feel sure there is one.'

Nell acknowledged the slick, sardonic interruption with a frown.

'Lucy didn't need saving.' Pity the same can't be said of me! She arched a brow and tilted her head up to him and found he was still watching her.

Nell swallowed as her stomach went into a slow-motion big-dipper dive.

'You told me that all along. How does it feel to be right?' She carried on talking because he wasn't saying anything and Nell felt an irrational need to fill the silence and avoid his smouldering stare.

The trouble with silence was you started thinking, and there were any number of things she didn't want to think about.

'I suppose you think it's funny?'

She struggled to put a name to his expression but it wasn't amusement.

'You're allowed to say I told you so,' she added. 'I bet you're just gagging to.'

'You want to know what I am…"gagging" to do, *querida?*'

'No!' Cheeks burning, she lifted her hands and held them to her ears.

His laughter took the edge off the high-voltage tension in the air.

'Look, let's forget the post-mortems, what's done is done, no point crying over spilt—'

'Milk?' he suggested, cutting across her.

Nell flushed. 'Well, anyway, that's it, then. Could you drop me off somewhere I can get a taxi to the airport on your way back?' Her smile faded. 'I'll never see you again.' Until he responded Nell wasn't even aware she had voiced the realisation.

'It is not impossible.'

The mortified colour rushed to her cheeks. 'Well, our paths are not likely to cross unless you come into the library to borrow a book.'

He lowered his glance with slow deliberation, causing Nell to lift her hands in a protective gesture across her stomach. 'Or you are carrying my child.'

Nell gave an embarrassed hollow laugh. 'That isn't going to happen.' Anyone would think, from the way he kept harking on about it, that he *wanted* it to happen.

'As you say, not likely, but I think we should stay in contact,' Luiz heard himself say.

'You do?' Why?

'Just in case—' Just in case I wake up in the night and nothing but you will stop the ache—as the thought formed a flicker of movement in the periphery of his vision made Luiz turn his head.

'There might be some delay in that lift to the airport.'

'Why?' Did he really just suggest that they stay in touch or had she imagined it? Did she really want to continue something with a man who carried so much emotional baggage?

'Because my sensitive, heartbroken cousin has just driven off in the car.'

'What?' Nell exclaimed, running across to the window in time to see a dust cloud. 'But he can't do that.'

CHAPTER ELEVEN

'HE HAS done that.'

'The little idiot!'

Luiz clicked his tongue in mock reproval. 'Is that any way to speak about a sensitive young man?' he chided.

Nell flashed him an irritated look. 'So what happens now?'

Luiz produced a mobile phone from his pocket. 'I use this and arrange us some transport. I suggest you use the time to freshen up.'

Nell lifted a self-conscious hand to her hair. 'I must look a wreck.'

'You look...' Nell watched a strange look spread across his face as he stared at her for what felt like a long time. 'You look fine.'

His manner was dismissive as he started punching numbers into his phone.

For want of anything better to do and glad of the opportunity to escape his unsettling presence, she set off in search of a bathroom.

The first door she tried was locked, the second was a bedroom with a connecting bathroom, big, luxurious, with an old-fashioned claw-foot tub that could have bathed an army. Had Luiz ever shared it?

She dismissed the intrusive question from her head. For

God's sake, the sooner she was out of Spain, the better—it was turning her into some sort of sex addict!

A glance in the mirror revealed that Luiz had been economical with the truth. Fine was one thing she did not look! A total wreck on the other hand? Yes, that definitely applied. So did scary, she thought, lifting a tangled strand of the hair that fell in witchlike tangles around her face, before dropping it with a grimace.

'Right, we can't do glamorous, but clean—or *cleanish* at least—we can do.'

Wetting her hands, she ran her fingers through her totally wild hair, smoothed her stained and creased clothes and grimaced at the result.

With a sigh she filled the basin with water and set about repairing some of the surface damage. The results were a slight improvement, though the dark mark on her cheek she spent ages scrubbing proved to be a bruise, not dirt.

'Well, that will have to do,' she told her reflection as she took a deep breath and left the room. She went directly to the drawing room but Luiz was no longer there. She was about to go in search of him when the sound of voices drew her to the window.

Luiz was standing in the driveway talking to a man about his own age. They were both standing beside a truck. The sight should have lifted her spirits—presumably this was her taxi. Instead to her bemusement Nell felt strangely downbeat.

Luiz turned his head, caught sight of her in the window and waved his hand for her to join them.

Outside the light breeze that blew in from the sea was pleasantly cool. It caught her damp hair and Nell needed both hands to anchor it from her face as she walked towards the two men.

They both stopped talking as she approached. The stranger smiled as Luiz introduced her.

'This is Francesco Angelus. He has ridden, or in this

case—' he flashed the other man a smile '—driven to our rescue.'

'It is nice to meet you, Miss Frost. Have you known Luiz long?'

Nell saw his eyes drift towards her finger and widen; she tucked it self-consciously behind her back and said with a composure she wasn't feeling. 'Not long.'

Luiz said something to the other man in Spanish, then, turning to her, added, 'I'm just going to close the cottage up. Wait here.'

Nell lifted her hand in a mocking salute and clicked her heels. 'Yes, sir!'

A smile slid into Luiz's eyes as he bowed his head in acknowledgement. '*Please* stay here.'

Francesco, who had watched this interchange with interest, waited until Luiz had vanished inside the building before he spoke.

'I'm glad that Luiz has brought someone here. It has been a long time. It was not healthy,' he mused, 'to make this place some sort of shrine.' He added something in Spanish, but the only word Nell caught was Rosa.

Nell, her brow furrowed in enquiry, turned to look at the tall Spaniard. If she had never met Luiz she would have classed him pretty much stunningly handsome, but her measure of male perfection had changed.

A lot of things had changed.

'This was actually,' he continued, casting a thoughtful glance towards the cottage, 'always more Luiz's place than Rosa's—too close to the home she wanted to escape. Rosa was a city girl at heart. She used to say the cosmopolitan buzz fed her artistic juices, though she loved the light in the studio here. For Luiz rebuilding the place virtually stone by stone when they first married was a labour of love—I helped out a bit.'

Nell's eyes widened in comprehension. She recalled his reluctance to enter and now she knew why: this had been the home he had shared with his wife.

'Even though everyone knows that Luiz will inherit when Doña Elena dies—'

'They do?' Nell felt uneasy, but thought it a strong possibility he was just quoting Luiz.

'Of course. Who else is there…Felipe?' Francesco suggested with a good-natured smile. 'It's just if he lost all his money tomorrow, a stretch I know, but if it happened I think if he had to choose one place, one piece of property, to keep intact I think it would be this place. Not worth much financially but it carries so many memories.'

'He doesn't come across as a sentimental man. You knew Rosa?'

Francesco's brows lifted. 'I'm her brother. I thought you knew.'

Nell's eyes fell. 'Sorry, no, I didn't.' The extent of her ignorance was becoming more obvious with each passing second, also the extent of her misjudgement. Could it be true? Had Luiz been telling the truth all along?

'Don't worry, I'm fine with you being here,' he added, clearly misinterpreting her discomfort. 'I've been telling Luiz for years now that he can't live in the past. He needs a woman and coming back here with you is obviously his way of laying old ghosts. You're obviously very good for him.'

Nell, blushing madly, shook her head. 'Not me, I'm not his woman, I'm…' She thought about the ring on her finger that felt like a burning brand and closed her mouth. Explanations were only going to make things look worse.

Francesco smiled, and taking her hand between the two of his, bowed slightly over it. 'Don't worry about me. I understand…'

You so don't, thought Nell.

'Your secret is safe with me.'

'No secret,' she promised, hardly daring to imagine what he was thinking.

'And when you're ready to go public I'll be the first to toast you both. Luiz is one of my favourite people, and I've a lot to thank him for, but you know Luiz—he runs a mile from gratitude and he doesn't like anyone to know about his good deeds.' His tone grew reminiscent as he continued. 'We grew up together, Luiz, Rosa and I. Our family had been tenants on the estate for generations. My father still has a farm near the castillo. I took over a vineyard about a mile away from here five years ago or so. Luiz's investment has meant—' He stopped abruptly in a manner guaranteed to excite Nell's curiosity, then finished, 'Let's just say I owe him.'

Nell listened to his confidences, her dismay growing.

'I always knew he would be successful, but the great thing about Luiz is he doesn't forget his old friends no matter how many billions he makes.'

Billions…? Before Nell opened her mouth to extract further details Luiz appeared.

'Are you ready to go?'

Nell, who hadn't heard his approach, turned and saw his dark gaze was trained on her hand still enfolded in Francesco's warm grip. The expression glowing in those dark depths was openly hostile.

Blushing, Nell pulled her hand away then immediately regretted her guilty response—she had nothing to feel guilty about, if of course you excluded a night of passion with a tall, dark stranger. She glared at Luiz and flashed a smile of particular warmth at Francesco.

'I was the one who was waiting,' she reminded him, thinking, Billionaire?

Francesco, oblivious to the undercurrents, smiled. 'I'll be

seeing you again very soon, I hope.' His smile included Nell as he clapped Luiz on the back.

Nell thought about the return journey alone with Luiz and her face dropped. 'Aren't you coming?'

'It's only a short walk back over the fields for me. Luiz will send the car back.' He caught Nell's hand, brushed the back of it with his lips in a courtly gesture and, with a wave, headed off in the direction he had indicated.

In the car Luiz waited for Nell to fasten her seat belt before he started the engine. He slid the car into gear, then with a muttered imprecation slid it into neutral and switched off the ignition.

Nell turned her head. 'Let me guess—we are out of petrol?'

He sketched a humourless smile. 'He's married.'

Nell looked at him blankly. 'What?'

'Francesco is married.'

She'd been slow to catch his drift, but now she had the angry colour flew to her cheeks. 'You are telling me this why?' She just wanted to hear him say it.

'Well, you were clearly very taken with him.'

She arched an ironic brow and fixed him with a cold glare. 'How charmingly put—much nicer than flat out accusing me of being a slut. It may surprise you to learn that I can smile at a man without ripping off his clothes.'

'You did not smile at me and you ripped my clothes off anyway.'

Nell drew a shuddering breath. I walked right into that one. 'I liked Francesco because he is a *gentleman*. You are a total *barbarian!*' She flung the accusation in a voice that ached with loathing.

She was actually shaken by the violent depth of her feelings. All her emotions seemed to be extreme around this man.

The fine muscles around his jaw tightened as their glances

locked, stormy dove-grey on smouldering brown. Sheer obstinacy prevented her shrinking back in her seat—he looked the barbarian she had accused him of being and more.

So why was her pulse racing in excitement? Nell asked herself, the voice in her head mocking her newfound taste for barbarians with beautiful mouths.

Nell's eyes flickered wide in horrified recognition.

Luiz held her eyes for one long nerve-shredding moment before switching on the engine, crunching the gears and grunting. 'Maybe you bring out the barbarian in me.'

CHAPTER TWELVE

IT WAS LATE afternoon when they reached the castillo; since the heated exchange when they had set out Luiz hadn't spoken a word.

And Nell had not felt inclined to initiate a conversation, as conversations, even ones that involved safe, boring subjects like the weather, somehow developed sexual undertones.

Why was everything suddenly about sex: the elusive fragrance of his warm body, the stubble on his chin, his damned stupidly long eyelashes? It was, she decided, one of life's great enigmas—either that or she had lost her mind.

So what happens now? Nell wondered, casting a surreptitious glance at Luiz's profile. In the shadows cast by the tall trees that lined the entire driveway it was impossible to make out details, just the strong, pure outline.

Would he put her in a taxi or expect her to share his bed?

A shiver shimmied down her spine as she slipped free of her safety belt and thought about the latter possibility—and if he did would she accept?

Would it be so terrible?

Nell's eyes flickered wide—the fact she had seriously asked herself the question even hypothetically meant there had been a major shift in her thinking over the past twenty-four hours.

It wasn't as if it could make things worse to sleep with him, in a bed—she would still be going home tomorrow. And she wanted him—why deny it when she couldn't think about anything else?

The acknowledgement of her total fixation drew a tiny grunt of shock from her dry throat.

Luiz, who had just switched off the engine, turned his head at the sound. 'Are you all right?'

'Fine, totally fine!' And then, because her cheery smile seemed to throw him, she pressed her hand to her chest and cleared her throat. 'I'm just a bit…dry. I'll be fine after a cup of tea…if you have…if it's not too much trouble,' she finished lamely.

He raised a brow and regarded her quizzically. 'You want tea?'

I want you. 'That would be good, please.'

Luiz carried on looking at her in that spooky way that made her feel he could actually see the thoughts in her head.

There were beads of sweat along her upper lip when she finally managed to break eye contact. The atmosphere in the car hummed with tension. 'Gosh, I'm so stiff it will be good to stretch my legs.'

Nell almost fell out of the car in her effort to escape. She stood there drawing in big shaky gulps of fresh air.

She had gone through her entire adult life without any sex and now she couldn't think about anything else!

Nell heard the crunch of gravel as Luiz got out and joined her; she didn't turn her head, but she knew he was standing behind her. The sensitive skin on the back of her neck prickled as she sensed his presence. She was painfully aware of Luiz, the texture of his skin, the sound of his voice… She closed her eyes—what was happening to her?

If anyone had told her twenty-four hours earlier that she would be unable to breathe because a man was standing close to her she would have laughed in her face.

This was ridiculous. Nell pinned a smile on her face, turned around and heard herself say with wince-inducing chirpiness, 'Well, we're here.'

'So we are.'

There was nothing chirpy about Luiz's voice. The low, seductive rasp sent her stomach muscles into violent quivering mode.

Standing there, one thumb hooked into the belt of his jeans, the breeze tugging at his dark hair, he looked totally relaxed until you reached his eyes. They were not relaxed, they were dark, smouldering with a raw, undisguised hunger.

The air between them shimmered thick with unspoken dark, smoky desires. Heat swirled through Nell as a violent stab of sexual longing nailed her to the spot, drawing the air from her lungs in one gasping breath, and she said the first thing that came into her head.

'Why didn't you tell me the cottage was your home? Yours and your wife's.'

'It did not seem relevant.'

Nell wasn't convinced by the careless shrug. 'It was the first time you'd gone back there.' She imagined him walking from room to room recalling the special memories they held and felt depressed. 'It's special to you.'

'It's a place.' Luiz was surprised to find he could say it and mean it. In a sense returning there had been liberating, it was something that he now knew he ought to have done years before.

'A special place.'

Her persistence began to visibly annoy him. 'What I did or felt before we met does not concern you, Nell.'

Nell blinked. Was Luiz saying that what he did and felt now did concern her? It was only the sound of someone clearing his throat that stopped her blurting out the question on the tip of her tongue.

Nell jumped at the sound, embarrassment swirling through her as she looked away. Talk about saved by the bell! She was guilty of reading far too much into his most casual remark—a case of hearing what she wanted to?

'Ramon?' Luiz struggled to hide his frustration and impatience as he turned to the other man.

Ramon slid a glance towards Nell and nodded, his manner pleasant and not, to her relief, particularly curious. The curiosity factor increased dramatically when his eyes brushed her ring. They jumped, startled, back to her face—you could almost hear him thinking, Odd choice for the man who could have anyone.

Oh, God, she was really going to have to get this thing off, she thought, tugging at it surreptitiously with more hope than expectation of feeling it loosen.

It stayed where it was.

'If I could have a word, Luiz?'

Luiz nodded to Nell and said, 'This won't take long.'

It couldn't. The journey here had been sheer hell. He'd barely been able to concentrate on the road ahead; his mind had kept drifting off and always in the direction that involved her skin, her softness, her mouth, on him, under him, around him.

Nell watched the men talk. She couldn't hear what they were saying. Had something happened to Luiz's grandmother? Had her condition taken a turn for the worse?

Luiz gave her no time to enquire when he returned, he just said abruptly, 'Go with Ramon. I will be with you later.' Then he was gone. Nell didn't even have a chance to challenge his assumption she would be waiting.

'Miss Frost.' The man with the warm eyes from yesterday explained that he was the estate manager and he would, he said, escort her to Luiz's private apartments.

Nell, feeling awkward, nodded and said, 'Call me Nell, please.'

'It is this way.' He stood to one side to allow her to join

him on the path that went in the opposite direction to the one that Luiz had taken. 'The castillo can be confusing until you get your bearings.'

Following him through the maze of corridors, Nell doubted that the day would ever come that she got her bearings even if she spent the rest of her life here, which she very obviously wouldn't.

This wasn't really happening; it was a dream. A defiant light entered her eyes. It was a dream she wanted to cram as much fantasy as possible into before she woke up. It wasn't that she was actively seeking a replay of last night's wild passion, it was just, if it happened—well, she wasn't going to actively resist it. She was going to go with the flow.

Do you want uncomplicated sex? Can you even *do* uncomplicated sex? asked the doubtful, disapproving voice in her head.

Nell accepted Ramon's invitation to step through the door into Luiz's private apartment. When the choice was uncomplicated sex or no sex at all the decision was easy to make because the truth was where Luiz Santoro was concerned she had no pride and even less common sense.

Bringing the internal debate to a halt, she said the necessary polite things to Ramon before he left her alone.

Alone meant the doubts really started creeping in; after a couple of nervous circuits of the sitting room she searched out a bathroom.

A couple of minutes later she was in the shower allowing the needles of hot water to wash away the dirt and soothe her bruises. She emerged feeling a lot fresher. The bruises remained, though, and a couple of spectacular scratches. She overcame her reluctance to put back on her creased clothes, but what choice did she have? He had to have something to take off, reasoned the voice in her head.

'Optimist,' she accused her image in the steamy mirror. Her grin faltered. 'You're taking a lot for granted, Nell Frost.

A few smouldering looks do not make a date. This is not the middle of the wilderness. A man has more options. There are other ways to spend an evening or an afternoon—there might be a good film on the TV,' she observed, only half joking.

The longer she was alone with her thoughts, the less realistic her rather shocking plans for a day of wild passion seemed.

She left the bathroom trying not to allow her thoughts or her eyes to stray to the quite incredibly large bed that dominated Luiz's bedroom.

Nell's rather tense expression relaxed into a smile when in the sitting room beyond she saw the tray of tea and sandwiches waiting for her—two cups, so obviously Luiz did plan to return some time soon.

After taking a sandwich and pouring herself a cup of tea she sat down on the leather sofa and waited.

She didn't have long to wait. When he entered the room her heart started banging violently against her ribs.

Luiz stopped dead when he saw her, his eyes drifting from her freshly scrubbed face to the cup of tea in her hands and on to her hair hanging wetly around her shoulders.

Nell felt relieved when he finally broke the simmering silence.

'You look so young.'

Nell wasn't sure from the accusing note in his voice if she was meant to apologise. Instead she said stupidly, 'Thanks for the tea.'

He nodded his head in acknowledgement. 'You're welcome.'

'I hope you don't mind—I used your shower.'

The only thing Luiz minded was that he had not been there to share the shower with her.

'Then you will smell better than me.'

In Nell's opinion there was nothing wrong with the way he smelt—nothing at all. She did not share this opinion but instead asked, 'Is your grandmother worse?'

He angled a brow. 'She is in good spirits. It was a call from my office that kept me.'

'You have an office?'

'Several.'

'You're rich?'

Luiz dug his hand into his pocket and shrugged; someone had clearly been talking. 'I am not poor.'

'The odd billion doesn't count, then,' she suggested in a quivering voice. When Luiz didn't correct her Nell swallowed and said, 'I thought Francesco was exaggerating.' Her eyes slid to the ring on her finger. 'So it wasn't about your grandmother's money? You were telling the truth all along.'

'Am I meant to apologise for not lying?' Was he lying to himself when he told himself yet again that this was just about sex? Luiz wasn't sure he was ready for that much truth yet, so he turned a deaf ear to the intrusive thought.

Nell put her teacup onto the tray and unfolded her legs. 'You could have told me,' she added angrily. 'You knew what I thought and you could have put me right at any point, but you enjoyed feeling superior.'

Nell saw the flash of surprised recognition in his eyes before he acknowledged the accusation with a shrug. 'You started off calling me a snake and your opinion went down from there. I suppose I was wondering just how low your opinion could go before it reached rock-bottom.'

She watched over the rim of her teacup as he perched on the edge of the window seat and, stretching his long legs out in front of him, crossed one ankle over the other.

'I still slept with you when I thought you were a snake.' Nell realised now that her determination to believe the worst of him had been in part a protective thing—she had wanted him to have a flaw, an ugly side that stopped him being perfect and irresistible.

This was not a discovery Nell planned on sharing with him.

Not now he had no flaws or ugly side and she had no protection. Because while not *quite* perfect—that would be boring—Luiz was, to her at least, totally irresistible.

His glittering gaze swivelled her way. 'So you did,' he drawled. 'And now that your opinion is perhaps not so low…?'

Nell's eyes slid from the dark glitter of sexual challenge in his bold stare. 'You look exhausted.'

'Someone kept me awake last night.' He was hoping she would do the same tonight. He had felt in need of her brand of comfort all day and it was driving him quietly out of his mind.

Nell cast him a look of reproach before she turned her attention to the original subject. 'When you said there was no money were you telling the truth then too?'

He looked startled. 'I said that?'

Nell, who recalled every word he had ever said to her, nodded.

'You really do have the uncanny ability to make me say things that should stay unsaid. Well, it's true. There is no money. The estate has not moved with the times, and Doña Elena took some bad advice financially.'

'The estate is in financial trouble?' Nell did not hide her surprise—nothing she had seen suggested straitened circumstances or neglect.

'There were problems and Ramon and I decided that it would be best not to trouble her with them. We arranged to have funds deposited in some accounts to cover the shortfalls and where necessary I made a few capital investments in renovation projects.'

It took a couple of seconds for her to process this casually delivered information. 'You mean, not only did you not want her money, you've been giving her yours for months.' Nell, who had thought she could not feel more stupid, discovered she could.

'It has been more in the nature of a long-term project.'

'Years!'

He acknowledged her startled suggestion with an inclination of his dark head before he dragged a hand across the dark shadow on his hair-roughened jaw.

'I wanted to save my grandmother the humiliation and heartache of losing the estate that has been her life. It seemed like the least I could do for her considering she has been mother and father to me after my parents dumped me on her for the holiday one year and never got around to picking me up. Understandable really,' he mused wryly. 'A weedy, sickly kid did quite frankly ruin their globetrotting social life.'

Nell struggled to get her head around Luiz as a sickly, unwanted child, and struggled even more to understand how any parent could just abdicate their responsibilities and their own child. She wondered how Luiz could recite the history without even a trace of visible bitterness.

'Though to be fair it was work for them—they make travel documentaries.'

Ah, there was the bitterness—he was human after all, and he was obviously totally devoted to his grandmother.

'I don't know how anyone could leave their own child.' Her jaw tightened as she found herself hating two people she had never met.

An expression she couldn't read flickered at the back of his hooded gaze, but it was not echoed in his flat tone as he said, 'I'm sure you can't, but not everyone has your sense of duty.'

Nell sprang to her feet, her expression passionately intense as she pressed a hand to her breast and cried, 'It's not about duty, it's about *love*.' Then, suddenly feeling painfully self-conscious, she sank back down muttering, 'People who don't know that shouldn't have children.'

He shrugged. 'They were and are very wrapped up in one another.'

Nell gave a contemptuous snort. 'They sound like selfish idiots to me.'

'I seem to recall you expressing a similar view about me.'

Her flushed face lifted to his. There was still a sparkle of indignation in her grey eyes. 'You are an idiot—sometimes,' she admitted. 'But you wouldn't let someone else bring up your child.'

The humorous glint faded from his eyes. 'No, Nell, I would not, but I would not give my wife the child she craved. I think that makes me worse than selfish.'

'It makes you human, you stupid man!' she exploded.

He raised his brows at the heat in her retort. 'I am considered pretty smart by most people.'

Nell sniffed. 'It just shows you how ridiculous people can be, then. Your wife died—it wasn't your fault, was it?' She watched the cold, closed look spread across his face and hated it.

'A car crash—she was travelling alone back from Barcelona.'

'Then *not* your fault,' she repeated. 'You're alive, Luiz.'

He inhaled deeply and suddenly felt this statement was truer than it had been for years. 'I am.'

Nell, her heart racing, watched him approach, her eyes fixed on the slow, deliberate tread of his polished shoes. He stopped about three feet away.

'Let me be straight with you.'

Her eyes lifted to knee level; her breathing had gone haywire.

'There are two ways this night could go.'

Her eyes reached chest level and stopped.

'Firstly, if you wish I could arrange transport to the airport, book you into a hotel for the night. Secondly, and I have to tell you this is my preferred choice, you spend the rest of the day and night here with me.'

She sucked in a deep startled breath as her eyes flew to his face. The heat and unvarnished desire in his made her gasp.

Luiz's eyes did not leave hers as he inclined his head towards the big bed visible through the open bedroom door and added in a throaty purr, 'In that bed.'

Nell's eyes slid towards the bed and back to Luiz, then back to the bed. She swallowed. Her heart was beating so hard he had to be able to hear it.

'I will not lie and say I feel things I do not, do you understand, Nell?'

Nell tore her eyes from the bed. She tried to push her hair from her eyes, but her hand didn't obey her command; a strange enervating weakness held her. She drew a fractured sigh. 'I understand.' She understood he didn't love her.

'And your choice?' While his attitude and shrug had a take-it-or-leave-it quality, there was nothing casual about the tension twitching the fine muscles around his mouth, or the febrile shudders she could see running through his greyhound-lean frame.

'I would like to spend the night here with you, in a bed.'

Nell, frustrated at not being able to see his expression because of the hand he lifted to his face, waited tensely for his response to her admission.

'Thank God!'

Nell's shoulders slumped in relief.

When his hand fell away the gleam of predatory male satisfaction in his eyes made her stomach muscles quiver violently. She watched her breath coming in uneven shallow gasps as he walked the remaining distance towards her looking big and dark and deliciously dangerous.

Nell was suddenly gripped by panic.

What have I done?

What am I doing?

He was standing so close now she could see the fine lines radiating from his incredible eyes. All she had to do was stretch out her hand to touch him, touch all that marvellous male hardness. Her fingers curled into a fist—God, but she wanted to touch him.

'Our bargain—'

'Having sex was not part of our bargain. *Madre de Dios!*' he growled. 'I am tired of the bargain. I suggest we throw the damned thing out of the window and start from scratch.'

'Yes, please.'

He looked at the hands that Nell held out, then, with a strangled cry, folded his long brown fingers over them and hauled her towards him until their bodies collided.

'You have not the faintest idea how glad I am you said yes to this option.' His lips brushed her eyelids and cheeks, moved over the curve of her throat before claiming her mouth in a hard, hungry kiss that left Nell breathless, dizzy and craving more.

'Show me?' she whispered, sliding her hands around his neck and pressing her body to his. 'Show me how glad you are, Luiz. Please…?'

The request drew a long shuddering sigh from Luiz. He curled his fingers around her chin and tilted her face up to his. Nell could feel he was shaking; she could feel the erotic imprint of his rock-hard erection against her belly.

'I will show you how it should be this time,' he promised thickly as he stroked her hair. 'Last time…' A spasm of regret contorted his lean features.

Nell tugged at the corner of his mouth gently with her teeth, their breaths mingling as she raised herself on tiptoe and whispered back fiercely, 'You have nothing to make up for, Luiz. You were perfect. It was perfect.' She pressed her lips to his and kissed him hard.

With a groan Luiz scooped her up into his arms and carried her through to the bedroom. Together they fell onto the bed in a sprawl of tangled limbs. With soft grunts, desperate moans and whispered endearments they tugged at each other's clothes with a clumsiness born of sheer desperation until they lay naked facing one another.

They both lay there breathing hard.

Nell's eyes, dark with desire, glittered like jewels as she ran her fingers along the abrasive, hard, angular curve of his cheek towards his mouth. She luxuriated in everything that made him male and hard and so utterly perfect.

'Your mouth is a sheer miracle.' A shaky little laugh left her aching throat as she conceded, 'The rest of you is not half bad either.'

Luiz didn't laugh back. His eyes were hypnotically dark and so hot she could almost see the flames dancing deep in the velvety depths as he took her fingertips and drew them into his mouth and sucked.

The erotic thrill shot down to her toes as she squeezed her eyes tight shut. Nell heard the low, almost feral moan and didn't actually connect it with herself, she wasn't herself, she was floating, and everything below her waist had melted.

He took her fingers from his mouth, kissed the tip of each one slowly before fitting his mouth to hers, catching the soft flesh of her pink inner lip between his teeth.

'I have been thinking about doing this all day,' he confided thickly.

'I've been thinking about this too.'

Her eyes squeezed tight as he slid his tongue inside, following the full curve of her lush lips before plunging in deeper. Luiz struggled to soften the bruising pressure; he wanted her so much that every nerve in his body ached.

'Oh, my God, Luiz!' she gasped when the kiss stopped.

He looked deep into her eyes and said thickly, 'You trust me to make this good for you.'

She didn't have to think about it. 'Totally,' she sighed.

The complete lack of reservation in her eyes touched Luiz in a place that no one had reached before. He raised himself over her, his dark eyes sliding over her slim, pale body, and his hand trembled as he brushed her hair back from her brow.

The tenderness brought tears to her eyes. Simultaneously

the dark passion in his face sent a shiver of anticipation down her spine. Nell's spine arched as he kissed his way slowly down her body, his tongue and lips sending her spinning out of control.

Her breath came in hoarse gasps as his attention shifted to more intimate areas. The skilful erotic caresses of his hands and lips sent her close to the fulfilment her body and soul craved, and then each time he drew back, until finally as she felt her throbbing body was on the brink of explosion he slid into her, shockingly, beautifully filling her, merging, becoming one with her.

She wrapped her hips across his and clung as he began to move. When he felt the first ripples of her climax Luiz closed his eyes, every muscle and sinew and nerve ending in his body screaming for release as he heard her hoarse cry and felt her come quick and hard, her soft wetness tightening rhythmically around him.

As he looked into her shocked, passion-glazed eyes he said thickly, 'Once more with feeling, *querida*.' And he began to move slowly, rocking his hips into her, touching her, lighting a slow-burning fuse with his body.

Luiz and the fuse exploded in unison and for a long, breathless moment Nell lost all sense of self; they were one.

'That was…perfect.'

'Perfect,' Luiz echoed, sounding, she thought sleepily, as shaken as she felt.

After the second time they made love Luiz fell into a deep sleep of total exhaustion with Nell curled up in his arms.

Sleep eluded her. Her overactive mind just wouldn't switch off and, anyway, who wanted to sleep when she could look at Luiz?

She drew back a little, pushing her head into the pillow and pushing her hair back from her face so that she could watch him sleep. She was mesmerised by his face. Emotion thickened the aching blockage in her throat as she stared, committing each strong angle and intriguing plane to memory. She was fascinated by every little detail: his fingers that had moved so sensitively over her skin; the sleek, powerful muscles of his shoulders, the frosty network of scars on his chest hidden by the swirls of dark hair. Would she ever know how he came by them?

He shifted restlessly in his sleep of exhaustion, murmuring something in Spanish, and Nell moved closer, throwing her hip across his as she moulded her body to his hard contours and whispered soothingly, her lips brushing his ear, 'Go to sleep, lover.'

She felt some of the tension that bunched Luiz's muscles relax as if at some subconscious level he had registered her whispered words.

There was a sense of release in not needing to hide her feelings as she stroked his hair from his brow. Then, without warning, his eyes opened. Her arm extended in a graceful arc, Nell froze as he seemed to look straight at her, but Nell knew he was nine parts asleep.

'Rosa.'

He said the one word, then closed his eyes, oblivious to the woman who lay rigid with silent tears of humiliation and anguish spilling from her eyes.

One word could change so much.

Had he been thinking of his dead wife while he made love to her? Nell's stomach clenched with revulsion at the thought.

She lifted his arm from her waist and rolled out from under it, pulling herself into a sitting position on the edge of the bed. She lifted a hand to her trembling lips and doubted she would ever be able to rid herself of the bitter metallic taste of humiliation in her mouth.

She had felt beautiful and special and comfortable in her own skin with him—able, he had convinced her, to be herself.

All that sweet, terrifying tenderness and now this. It was like seeing heaven and plunging back to a cold, stony earth.

She sniffed and, pulling a sheet off the bed, wrapped it around her shoulders. Her quivering lips firmed. There was no way she could compete with a ghost, she didn't want to! Her mistake had been thinking—a classic case of seeing what you wanted—that it had been more than just sex for Luiz.

CHAPTER THIRTEEN

NELL checked the baby monitor was switched on and sat back down to read her book, the same page for the tenth time and it still hadn't sunk in. The exploits of her favourite female detective could not distract her from the introspective gloom of her own reflections. Any more than her brother and sister-in-law's boast that her nephew never woke once he was put down to sleep had saved her from having to go up and down the stairs four times.

She knew of course that she was going to have to snap out of it at some point, she was going to have to shrug it off and get on with her life, but that point had not yet arrived.

She had gone through a lot of soul-searching before she had written that letter to Luiz. A man deserved to know he was going to be a father, even though life would have been a lot simpler from her point of view if he had remained in ignorance.

Having Luiz in her life even in a peripheral part-time-father sort of way was not going to be easy—actually it was going to be hell. In fact the mental image of him strolling in with some gorgeous blonde on his arm to do the duty-dad thing had almost stopped her putting the letter in the post. God, but at times a conscience was a really inconvenient thing to possess.

Ironically, of course, her soul-searching had been a total waste of time. She had posted the letter a month earlier so, even allowing for the vagaries of the postal service, he had to have received it by now and so far his response had been a deafening silence.

Nell told herself she was relieved. She was angry not because he had shown extreme bad manners—in no world, not even his rich glamorous one, was it acceptable to file the letter along with, for all she knew, the other 'I'm carrying you child' missives that arrived on his desk—but because she had thought he would reply. She had *believed* he would; she had believed in him and his integrity. Now she knew she was a fool.

The disillusionment went deep.

Giving up on the book, she switched on the TV, turning down the volume to an inaudible murmur as she flopped back down onto the sofa.

She had been home for two weeks when she had made herself do the pregnancy test, or rather tests—she had done three before she accepted the result. Yet still it had not sunk in for a few days; she had walked around in a state of wilful denial. The sort of 'ignore it and it will go away' mentality that she had always thought cowardly in others—it turned out she was the biggest coward of all time.

It had hit home in, of all places, the waiting room at the dentist's surgery. She had been there for a check-up when the dentist had decided she was due a routine X-ray. The magazine she had picked up while she waited had opened on one of the typical 'celebrities living a life the rest of you can only dream of' double-page spreads during a glittery charity auction in New York.

She had recognised several famous faces and there had been Luiz, the only one not smiling but still managing to look more Hollywood and more sternly beautiful than any of them with his hand on the waist of a young Oscar-winning actress.

If the actress had been acting the adoration she had been looking up at him with she definitely deserved her Oscar, because Nell for one believed it.

It was crazy that such a silly thing should have brought the reality and the total impossible nature of her situation home to Nell, but it had.

In a perfect world, realising that you were in love with the man whose baby you carried should be a good moment, a moment to treasure. For Nell it had felt as though a very tall building had just fallen on her head, but the light at the end of the tunnel had been the realisation she wanted this baby, she would fight to have this baby—his baby.

Tears streaming down her cheeks, she had walked to the reception and mumbled, 'Sorry, but I can't have an X-ray. I'm pregnant.' Then before the startled-looking receptionist could respond she had fled. It was a shame—really good dentists were hard to come by and there was no way she was walking back into that building.

Pushing aside the memories and recalling the mantra she repeated to herself at frequent intervals extolling the advantages of single parenthood, she turned up the volume just as a quiz-show host with strangely orange skin appeared on the screen to the sound of thunderous applause.

With a wince she flicked the channel over and, drawing her knees up to her chin, she told herself it could be worse: she could be a guest at the party at her sister's house to celebrate her brother and sister-in-law's wedding anniversary.

When there had been a last-minute hitch with the babysitter, for once she hadn't been irritated by her sister's assumption she would step into the breach.

'Nell won't mind at all.'

For once Nell actually wouldn't, but it would, she reflected, have been nice to be asked.

'God, Nell, you're a total life saver,' her sister-in-law, Kate, said, adding anxiously, 'Are you sure you don't mind? The agency might be—'

'You don't want to leave Stevie with a stranger, Kate.'

Kate flashed Nell a look of apology. 'No, of course not, Clare, but—'

'Nell will be the only one there without a partner—'

'Actually, Clare, I invited Oliver Loveday. He's the new partner at the—'

That settled it for Nell. 'No, Kate, I'd love to babysit and, anyway, I've nothing to wear.'

Nell gritted her teeth while both women laughed as though she had made a hilarious joke.

'Nell thinks fashion is a new tee shirt.'

'And jeans that are only one size too big.'

'Two sizes if they're your hand-downs, Clare,' Nell added innocently. She saw her sister's lips tighten. Clare's struggle with her ever-expanding hips was well known and she felt a bit of a bitch. She didn't mind exactly being the butt of their humour, but she couldn't help but feel slightly resentful that it had never occurred to either of them that she might enjoy fashion had she ever had the money to spend on clothes.

A knock on the door shook Nell from her brooding reflections. She considered ignoring it, then thought about little Stevie upstairs waking up, the thought was enough to send her surging to her feet. It had taken her half an exhausting hour last time to settle the youngster, who looked cherublike and angelic when he was asleep. The problems started when he woke up. Even when he'd seemed soothed the cranky youngster had produced heart-wrenching tears every time she had tried to tiptoe out of the room.

'All right, all right,' she muttered, catching a slipper with her toe and hooking it back onto her bare foot—you didn't dress up for babysitting and Nell's slouchy outfit was intended for comfort. 'I'm coming, keep your hair on.'

She unlatched the front door and, leaving the chain attached, pulled it open a crack. Despite the fact her brother lived in an area where the most serious crime reported was someone picking the flowers in the square he had given her a strict lesson on security before he'd left. His son's life, he had reminded her severely when she had laughed, was in her hands.

Nothing was in her hands when the tall sinister shadow stepped forward into the security light; she fell gracefully onto her bottom where her limbs and appendages continued to disregard the instructions from her brain—which were along the lines of run…hide.

In the moment before she drew back with a gasp he had seen her eyes widen in shock. He could empathise if not sympathise with her reaction, which could not in his view come close to the shock he had suffered when he had opened the letter. His fingers curled over the envelope in the pocket of his coat when he heard the thud followed by sinister silence.

'Nell…Nell!'

Luiz inserted his fingers into the crack between the door and the frame feeling for the chain, his hand steady despite the adrenaline pumping through his veins in a torrent.

Even if she had wanted to respond to the urgent call of her name or the subsequent flood of angry-sounding Spanish she couldn't have; shock had totally paralysed her.

Was she injured? Speculation of the possibilities was a luxury he could not allow himself as he finally forced the chain. In moments like this imagination was not a useful thing.

The door swung inwards on the unoiled hinges with a creak worthy of a horror film. Luiz felt a rush of relief tempered by apprehension as he stepped inside and almost fell over a Victorian umbrella stand complete with umbrellas and into the hallway.

He took in the situation at a glance and reacted despite

Nell's feeble attempt to fend him off with her hand as he dropped down onto his knees beside her.

'Go away, I'm fine!' She lifted her head, felt her world swim and let it fall back. 'Stop doing that!' The clinical, detached explorative movement of his hands over her body evoked a less than clinical reaction from her nervous system.

'There doesn't seem to be anything broken.'

That's all you know, she thought, thinking of her poor heart that felt as though someone had ripped it out of her chest and stamped on it.

'Just give me a minute,' she said, closing her eyes. 'What?' As he hefted her into the air in one smooth motion, her face tucked underneath his chin, she produced a token kick but otherwise made no attempt to sabotage his rescue attempt.

A few moments later she was stretched out full length on her brother's sofa, a cheesy voice in the distance asking if she wanted to *take a risk?*

No risks—she was playing it safe from now on.

Nell struggled to raise herself. 'Will you switch off that thing?'

Luiz placed his hand lightly on her chest and she slumped back with a sigh. 'Stay still. You fainted.'

And whose fault was that? Nell hit his hand and raised herself up on her elbow. 'I have never fainted in my life. Go away!' She batted away his restraining arm and swung her legs out over the side of the sofa before hauling herself into a sitting position.

'See…I'm totally fine,' she snarled, pushing aside the strong and disturbing recollection of being scooped into his arms and cradled against a chest that had about as much give as steel but felt warmer and smelt quite frankly…gorgeous.

Luiz, a nerve pumping wildly in his lean cheek, folded his arms across his chest and said with a 'what are you going to do about it?' smile, 'I am not going anywhere, Nell. I have only just arrived.'

'What,' she demanded crankily as she pushed the silky wisps of hair from her eyes and fixed him with an unfriendly glare, 'are you doing here anyhow?'

She tried to look away but she couldn't; despite his negligent pose she could almost see the tension humming through his lean body.

A soundless sigh left her lips as she stared up at him. He looked utterly compelling in a dark, mean, moody sort of way. Under the sweep of his ludicrously long curling lashes his obsidian eyes glittered, reflecting back her own image, his mouth curled cynically down at one corner, the nerve beside it throbbing.

He shrugged off the full-length drover-style double-breasted raincoat he wore over his suit. It glistened with rain, as did his dark hair.

'I was looking for you.'

And now he had found her and he couldn't stop staring. His memory had not, as he had been telling himself, embellished the details—her eyes really were that big, her mouth that soft and kissable.

Nothing in his expression revealed the helpless lustful surge of his body or the fact he felt as though he were burning up from the inside out as he stared at her mouth, but he had no control over the dark dull lines of colour that emerged along the slashing angles of his cheekbones.

'How are you feeling?' He was relieved her scary pallor had receded, but she still looked incredibly fragile; it shocked him deeply to see how much weight she had lost.

Nell ignored the question. It would have been impossible to answer anyway—there were no words to adequately describe the cocktail of emotions churning inside her.

'Looking for me?' Despite her intention to stay cool and not allow him to guess how much he had hurt her, Nell couldn't stop the bitterness and resentment creeping into her voice as she added with a tight smile, 'Not with any great urgency.'

She watched through the inadequate protection offered by her lashes as an inexplicable expression of outraged incredulity flickered across his dark, stern features.

'You thought I ignored the letter?'

His indignation struck Nell as the height of hypocrisy. 'You did ignore it.'

'I didn't ignore it. I did not receive it.'

Nell, her lips curled into a contemptuous smile, shrugged and said, 'If you say so.'

His jaw clenched. 'I do say so.'

'It really doesn't matter to me one way or the other,' she lied.

'Yes, I can see that.'

The drawled sarcasm brought Nell's flashing eyes to his face.

'You addressed your letter to the castillo?'

A flicker of uncertainty entered Nell's eyes. 'I sent it to the castillo…so what if I did?'

'So I wasn't there. If it had been marked urgent it would have been forwarded to me, but as it was simply marked personal it sat there waiting for my return. My grandmother's health is much improved —incidentally she would, I am sure, send you her love if she knew I was here. I have been travelling. I only returned to Spain this morning.'

The memory of opening the letter and reading her curt, concise little note was one he could not relive without growing pale. She had given him all the relevant details datewise, but not a word of emotion had crept in. Not a single clue of whether she was sad, happy or indifferent to the news—whether she was sad, happy or indifferent to him.

The latter question was now less of a mystery. When she looked at him none of the above was evident; it was a contemptuous loathing that shone like a beacon in her wide-spaced clear eyes.

Nell's brows drew together as she gave a concessionary shrug. It was just feasible he was telling the truth. Jet lag would explain the high-tension aura he was exuding—that and learning he was about to be a father, which clearly had not had him breaking open a bottle of champagne.

'I'm glad your grandmother is feeling better.'

'As am I.'

Nell ignored the raw interjection and admitted casually, 'I saw a picture of you in New York.' She looked at him and thought, The day I realised I loved you.

'I had several business meetings there.'

An image of the actress with the paint-on white gown flashed into her head and Nell retorted, 'This wasn't a business meeting.' Then, conscious that her comment might be interpreted as jealousy, she added quickly, 'So you got home and read my letter.'

'I did.'

'I'm sorry.'

He flashed her an incredulous look. '*You* are sorry?'

Luiz stared at her. He was the one that ought to be apologising; to his way of thinking ignorance was no excuse. The thought of her coping with everything alone was like an icy hand in his chest.

He should have been there. He nearly had been there. If he hadn't been too damned proud to chase after her. For the first time in his life a woman had walked away from him and Luiz had not allowed himself to follow her. Instead he had nursed his resentment and tried to act—not well, as it happened—as though nothing had happened.

She shrugged and reached across to flick off the TV. 'Well, it couldn't have been the best coming-home present.'

His shuttered expression told her nothing, but it did not escape her notice that he didn't claim to be delighted. Instead he said quietly, 'It was always a possibility.'

'A pretty remote one. There was really no need for you to hotfoot it here—your reputation is safe.' The photo of him in New York had clearly been considered something of a scoop by the magazine that had identified Luiz as 'the thirty-two-year-old Spanish billionaire bachelor who guards his privacy zealously.'

She supposed it was natural for someone in his position to want to avoid too much publicity.

'I'm no more anxious to advertise this than you, so relax— I'm not about to blab about it to anyone, and anyway,' she added, placing a hand on her still-flat stomach, 'I'm not showing yet. Nobody suspects a thing, though Kate thinks I've taken the dieting too far.'

Luiz felt the anger lick through him. 'You think that is why I am here? You think I am here to stop you selling a kiss-and-tell tabloid story?'

His anger bewildered her. 'Well, why else would you jump on the first plane?'

'I have a private jet.'

'Of course you do,' she drawled, struggling to cloak her feelings behind a mask of cynical amusement.

'I clearly have a better opinion of you than you do of me.' Luiz stopped and rotated his head as if to relieve the tension in his shoulders, his ribcage lifting visibly as he inhaled deeply. Nell found she could not take her eyes off the thin white line of fury that outlined his finely sculpted sensual lips.

She could see he was furious though the why was still something of a mystery to her.

'It did not even cross my mind,' he continued in a voice that held an audible rasping tremor of emotion, 'that you would demean yourself by making money out of a revenge story.'

'Oh! Well, good, because I wouldn't. So why did you come, then?'

'*Why?*' His brow furrowed and he repeated in the same oddly flat tone, '*Why?* You are carrying my child, you are alone, I had no idea how you were coping or if you were well, which,' he added, his narrowed gaze sweeping her face, 'you clearly are not. I may be the sort of irresponsible fool who has unprotected sex, but I am not the sort of irresponsible fool who ignores his responsibilities.'

The admonishment brought a rush of colour to Nell's skin. She narrowed her eyes and thought, Suddenly he's the victim—great! 'Lucky me, I'm a liability. I feel better already.'

He looked at her in exasperation. 'You know that is not what I mean.'

'I know exactly what you mean and for the record I'm not your responsibility.' I want to be your love, you stupid man. Appalled at how close she had come to voicing her thought, Nell lowered her eyes and bit her lip. She was going to have to take more care in future; thinking before she opened her mouth would be a good start.

He arched a brow and visibly struggled to contain his annoyance. 'And I suppose the baby is not my responsibility either.'

Nell pursed her lips mutinously and said, 'No.' She ignored his hissing intake of exasperation and asked. 'How did you know I was here anyway?'

'I had the address of your sister's house.'

'I was in between addresses at the time I wrote the letter.' It sounded less emotive than temporarily homeless. 'And I have my own place now.' Nell smiled the sort of casual, confident smile that a woman with her *own* place would have, and luckily he had not seen her *own* place.

Staying with her sister had been a real incentive to Nell to find another place—*any* place. The atmosphere had not been pleasant. Clare had been furious that Nell had vanished just when, as she put it, 'all the work needed doing.' She had been even less pleased when Nell had refused to explain where she had been.

Nell, exhausted by the constant probing had eventually lost it and in the ensuing shouting match had called her sister a control freak. This had not gone down well, especially as Clare's husband Clive had inserted a dry, 'You're only just realising that, Nell?' into the heated discussion.

The atmosphere was still a little strained.

'You went to Clare's.' Her eyes flickered to his face. 'There's a party.'

'I noticed.' He had also noticed that Nell was absent from this family occasion.

Nell tried to imagine what impression Luiz had made walking into the party and her imagination failed her.

'That's how you knew I was here—they told you?' Nell could not hide her skepticism. It hardly seemed likely that her family would give her whereabouts to a total stranger, but then Luiz was a stranger who could be awfully persuasive and people did not as a rule say no to him.

She certainly hadn't.

Luiz watched her fluctuating colour and struggled to channel his driving need and lust—it was driving him to distraction—into a more practical and less frustrating direction. Should he call a doctor?

Before he could voice the suggestion she suddenly lost all colour. 'Lie down.'

Ignoring his urgent direction, Nell groaned as an awful possibility occurred to her. 'Please tell me you didn't tell them I was pregnant?' Nell knew she would have to break the news at some point, but she wanted it to be a time of her choosing.

'It was not the first subject we discussed.'

Nell gave him a level look.

'No, I did not tell them you are pregnant.'

Nell's relief was short-lived.

'But if you are expecting support from them when you do I would not hold your breath. From my observation they are crass, selfish, insensitive and utterly thoughtless.' Luiz smiled with grim satisfaction as he recalled the looks on their faces when he had told them what he thought of a family who dumped their responsibilities on the shoulders of a young sister and as far as he could see were still doing so.

Their faces had been pictures, not immediately of guilt— that had come after he had dispensed with their faltering and predictable excuses.

Nell could not argue with the essential accuracy of his rather brutal analysis, but she didn't feel he had a right to express it and she told him so.

'That's my family you're talking about. Do you always bad-mouth people behind their backs?'

'Oh, I bad-mouthed them to their faces.' Pleased to see that some more of the colour had returned to her cheeks, he leaned across and, with a finger under her chin, closed her mouth with a click. 'Where is the kitchen? Can I get you a glass of water?'

Nell looked at him uncertainly. 'You are joking, right?'

'I am capable of getting you a glass of water.'

'You said that to my s-sister and my brother a-and—'

'You are equally to blame, of course,' he observed, cutting across her.

'What do you mean?'

'Why are you here babysitting while they are enjoying themselves?'

'I offered,' she lied.

He looked unconvinced. 'Do you intend to play Cinderella all your life?'

'I don't!' she exclaimed.

His lips curled into a scornful smile. 'What are you doing waiting for a fairy godmother to appear? Or is it Prince Charming?'

'Well, if I was I certainly backed the wrong horse with you!' she shot back, still not sure whether he was being serious about what he had said to her family. 'Did you really crash the party?'

'I knocked and I was invited in by your niece.'

'You saw Lucy?' Her niece had come home from university for the weekend; some might think she had been the obvious candidate to babysit her little cousin.

Nobody had asked Lucy because Lucy would have said no. Maybe Luiz had a point? The private concession made Nell feel uncomfortable—had she become the family doormat?

No wonder he was looking at her with such irritation. He was probably comparing her with her confident, self-assured, beautiful niece whom nobody would dream of dumping on.

'I saw her.'

'And you liked her?' Silly question—what was not to like? Lucy was tall, blonde, bright and beautiful. The line of thought came to an abrupt halt as Nell realised with a sick feeling of disgust that she was jealous of her own niece!

The question seemed irrelevant to Luiz.

'I did not give it much thought.'

He thought about her now, and got the impression of tall and blonde, a younger version of her mother; the brother too was similar. The bland features of neither woman had made a lasting impression on him—he could walk past both in the street and not recognise either.

'You,' he said directing his gaze to Nell, 'do not look like your family.'

It was not the first time the dissimilarity had been noted; normally she accepted philosophically the recognition that she had got the short end of the genetic stick. That wasn't the situation now.

'I'd like to say I got the brains and they got the good looks, but actually they're quite smart.' It was a joke that had worked before; it did not now.

Luiz shook his head, exasperation and annoyance flickering in his eyes.

'Who put it into your head that you are not attractive?'

Nell regarded him with a baffled frown. 'I don't know what you're talking about.'

'I know you don't—that's what makes it so incredible.' Before Nell had an inkling of his intention he cupped her chin in one hand, his long fingers curling around her cheek as he turned her face first in one direction and then the other.

Nell almost tipped over into open panic as she endured his searching scrutiny. The brush of his fingers on the downy skin of her cheek made her tremble and intensified the string-dragging sensation low in her pelvis.

'You are and, with those bones, always will be a beautiful woman.'

'I'm not—'

'Shut up!' To ensure his growled command was obeyed he bent his head and fitted his mouth to her lips.

Nell opened her mouth and felt his tongue move against hers. She moaned into his mouth as desire, hot and thick, exploded in her veins. Her arms around his neck, she kissed him back with all the need and passion that had been locked inside her over the last weeks.

When they broke apart Luiz stayed close, his forehead resting on hers, their noses almost grazing, his breath warm on her cheek. She wanted the moment of intimacy to last for ever.

'I do not wish to hear any more about your beautiful family. They bore me.'

CHAPTER FOURTEEN

NELL couldn't help but smile to hear her family called boring. 'I do feel beautiful now.' She felt wild, abandoned and totally irresistible, but then that was what Luiz's kiss could do.

The admission drew a husky laugh from Luiz as he straightened up.

Nell's smile evaporated as he began to shrug off his jacket. She could see that some men might construe a kiss as an invitation, especially that kiss, but this was not something she could allow to happen.

'What do you think you're doing?' Nell asked, feeling things shift inside her as she stared. The fabric of his pale-coloured shirt was fine, suggesting at the defined ridges of his flat belly.

Luiz smoothed down the fabric of the jacket he had draped over the back of a chair and looked unperturbed by the aggressive hostility in her manner. 'My clothes are wet.'

'Oh!'

Nell was aware she ought to be feeling relief that she had misread his intentions, but disturbingly that emotion was not uppermost.

It was insane, but part of her had actually wanted to stop thinking, wanted to stop being level-headed; part of her had wanted to be carried away by the blind driving passion of the moment. Part of her had wanted him to take his clothes off.

Part of her still did.

At the tone of her voice Luiz turned his head; the furrow of puzzlement vanished and he laughed.

Nell was too embarrassed that he could read her thoughts so well to notice the strained, forced quality in his laugh.

'Relax, I won't take anything else off. Unless you ask me to.'

Nell's startled gaze flew to his, connected with the bold, suggestive heat in his smouldering stare. Her heart thudding, she looked away. 'In your dreams.'

The calculated insolence of his smile guttered at her words.

His jaw clenched as his lashes came down over his glittering gaze.

'I prefer reality to dreams.'

Luiz had become used to waking from the dreams that tormented him nightly, desire and arousal pumping through his veins, choking with the grinding, aching frustration that stayed with him all through the day, left him edgy, short-tempered and not enthused by the idea of going to sleep.

'The weather is terrible today.'

'Good choice—as classic safe subjects go the weather is always right up there. Though while we're on the subject I'm not sure you'd be any drier in your flat than outside.'

Luiz had been appalled to see the condition of the one-bedroom apartment on the top floor of the building that faced a busy main road. Anything *less* suitable for a baby would have been difficult to find.

'The landlord has promised to fix the roof before…' Nell heard herself say defensively. She stopped and looked at him. 'You have seen my flat?' she added sharply.

'Well, obviously I went there first.'

Her mind raced with hysterical conspiracy theories. 'How did you know where I was living?'

'I picked up a phone and asked someone to find out,' he explained, his calm manner making her feel slightly foolish.

'Delegation,' he observed with a humourless smile, 'is a marvellous thing. It did not require the services of the FBI. You can, of course, not stay there.'

Nell who had only ever intended the flat as a stopgap, narrowed her eyes and lifted her chin in response to the high-handed edict.

'I'd say that is none of your business. If I want to live in a tent at the bottom of the garden, I will.' Though clearly not with her brother's blessing, his prize-winning hydrangeas were the love of his life.

She saw no need to share this information with Luiz, who obviously if given an inch would take half a continent! Her life had already spiralled so far out of her control that she zealously guarded the few areas she could still influence.

Luiz looked at her through dark narrowed eyes and she thought for a moment he was going to argue the point so it was something of an anticlimax when he shrugged and said calmly, 'As you wish. The question of where you will live will obviously be academic shortly.'

'How do you figure that?' she called after him as he vanished in the direction of the kitchen.

He returned a moment later carrying a glass of water. Nell, her chin propped on her knees, watched him, her stomach flipping helplessly in response to the animal grace and sheer elegance of his simplest movement.

'Well, why will it be academic?' she asked, taking the glass from him while taking immense care not to allow her fingers to brush his. Her efforts drew a small wry smile from him, which she pretended not to see.

'Well, once we are married you will hardly be living in a garret.'

Only Luiz's spookily swift reflexes prevented the water spilling all over Nell and her brother's new sofa. Nell murmured, 'Thank you,' as she watched him place it safely on a coffee table. 'It's just I thought for a minute you said *married*.'

Luiz, who loosed his tie and lowered his long-limbed frame onto the arm of a chair beside her, did not join in her laughter.

'I did.'

'I think you're suffering from jet lag.'

'I told you before that I would honour my responsibilities.'

'And you think that involves marrying me. Leaving aside the small point of a girl liking to be asked…' He looked at her blankly and she said, 'Has it even crossed your mind that I might say no?'

His expression made it pretty obvious it had not.

'That I might have other plans that don't include you?'

The suggestion drew a dark frown from Luiz. 'You are saying there is another man in your life?'

Nell rolled her eyes; how like a man. 'Why does it always have to be about a man? Has it crossed your mind that a woman can live a perfectly full life without a significant other half? And anyway, for all you know I might want to make up for lost time and play the field!'

The images that flashed through Luiz's head brought a metallic taste of utter repugnance to his mouth. 'No!'

Her brows went up. 'I beg your pardon?' she said in a low, dangerous voice.

Luiz irritably swatted the beads of sweat that had broken out over his brow with the back of his hand and said, 'A trail of one-night stands are not the male role models I had in mind for my child.'

This from the man she had seen with a half-naked woman draped all over him in a magazine and she was betting that they hadn't spent the night in separate rooms. Nell felt her temper climb as her thoughts dwelt on the blonde actress.

'So all of a sudden it's *your* child, is it? Well, for the

record, you're not the male role model I had in mind for my child. As for my sex life, I'll conduct it when I have one with more d-decorum and discretion than you, Luiz Santoro!' Breathing hard, she sank back into the sofa and fought off the strong desire to burst into tears.

'What have I done?'

'I saw the...'

A flash of comprehension relaxed the lines of tension in his face. 'You saw the article, the photo of me with Sarah.'

'I might have.'

'You really have no need to be jealous—that was just a photo opportunity and Sarah has a film to promote.'

Good for Sarah, bless her silicone-enhanced bust, Nell thought viciously.

'You think I'm interested in your sex life!' She loosed a slightly manic laugh and sneered. 'You can sleep your way through the cast of every daytime soap for all I care. Dear God, I only mind that you seem to imagine just because I showed no damned restraint with you it means I'm a sitting duck for every man who deigns to notice I'm f-female. It's going to take more than a man saying he wants me to make me lie back and think of E-England!'

Her shaky postscript caused the explosive anger that had been visibly building on Luiz's face during her rant to dissolve.

From Nell's point of view what replaced it was a lot more worrying.

'And if I said I wanted you?'

Nell closed her eyes on the male speculative gleam in his. God, she really had lost her mind. Now, with all that had happened, she still wanted him so much that it was a physical pain. She knew that if he touched her, if he kissed her again, her resolve would dissolve.

The knowledge was terrifying. She swallowed, her glance

lingering on his hands and his long, tapering fingers. Her eyes darkened and a fractured sigh left her lips as she recalled those fingers moving over her skin. For long seconds she was paralysed by a wave of longing.

Several soothing breaths later she regained the use of her vocal cords. 'I'd say don't waste your breath. Been there, done that, got the maternity smock!'

Instincts of self-preservation had made her strike out, but as she watched the colour drain from his face as her jibe found its target Nell felt no triumph.

'I understand that you're angry with me.'

'I'm not angry with you, I'm angry with me!' she exclaimed.

Luiz studied her, his curiosity clear, and asked, 'Why?'

Nell just looked back at him and shook her head. What was she meant to say—I'm angry because I love you? I'm angry because I'm seriously tempted to take what's on offer?

'I think when you stop and think about this without the emotion—'

'Without emotion!' she echoed, shaking her head as she saw red. 'The day I think about marriage without emotion is the day I have a personality transplant! Will you listen to yourself, Luiz? Marriage is *about* emotion. It's about love and commitment. I may be pregnant but that doesn't mean I have to settle for second best.

'The day I settle for second best is the day I…' She shrugged and shook her head. 'It's just not going to happen. I think my child deserves better.' The heat died from her face as she lifted her eyes to his and asked simply. 'Can you offer me better, Luiz?'

'I can offer you a home where our child will be brought up with parents who are committed to one another.'

Nell's eyes fell from his. She supposed she ought to be grateful he wasn't pretending to feel things for her he clearly didn't, but at that moment being thankful that even after she had virtually begged he was unable to say he loved her was beyond her ability.

'If I agreed to this I would have to be committed—it's madness, Luiz. Look, I know you're trying to be noble and everything,' she admitted.

'And you think you should be punished or something…' That was coming across strongly. 'Well, I can't help that. Go jump in an icy lake, give your money to charity if it salves your conscience, but I have to tell you,' she added in a shaky voice, 'that the idea of marriage to me being a penance is not all that flattering.'

He regarded her with deep frustration and resisted the childish impulse to tell her that there were women out there who would not consider themselves certifiable if they were to accept his proposal of marriage. That there were women out there who had worked very hard to make him say the words *marry me*.

But he realised that telling Nell she didn't know how lucky she was might not be a wise move. It would also give her the ammunition to call him vain, self-satisfied and any other insults that came to mind.

She might also be right.

'Why do you purposely misinterpret everything I say and do?'

Nell, who translated this complaint as 'why don't I agree with everything you say?' shrugged. 'What can I say? It's a gift.' She anchored her hair behind her ears and, leaning across, took the glass from the coffee table. She wasn't thirsty, but she needed the breathing and thinking space.

He watched her, his expression brooding as she raised it to her lips and gulped.

'I could point out the impracticalities of your bringing up a child alone.'

Nell returned his direct look. 'You could,' she agreed in a voice that gave no clue to her racing pulse.

'Or I could fight you for custody?'

He watched the colour fade from her face and regretted his taunt. His eyes fell from hers. 'Though I don't think that will be necessary.'

'Or wise,' she tacked on seamlessly.

His glance swept upwards and connected with the challenging glitter of her eyes. Holding his gaze, Nell got to her feet and stood there, her hands on her hips, looking, he thought, as proud as a queen for all her baggy sweat pants, tee shirt and that ridiculous cardigan that swamped her.

Through his extreme annoyance a surge of admiration surfaced. Nell Frost was the most obstinate woman he had ever met, but she had guts and an inner toughness that were at variance with the air of extreme fragility more pronounced since her recent weight loss. A frown twitched his eyebrows above his hawkish nose when he recalled how light she had felt in his arms, her bones like a bird. He struggled to make sense of the mixture of lust and protective tenderness that accompanied the recollection.

He didn't love her. A man could only have one love in his life and he had had his, he reminded himself bleakly, yet the tenderness, the fierce, inexplicable protectiveness, the constant nagging ache of desire in his loins... How could he analyse his feelings for this woman? His thoughts were interrupted by a constant static buzz of emotional interference.

Nell regarded him with cold contempt and warned, 'If you try to take my baby you'll have a fight on your hands. I don't care if you have all the money in the world!'

The determination in her voice made Luiz want to applaud. This woman was irrational, totally unreasonable, but she was a fighter.

He spread his hands in a pacifying gesture. 'I am a lover, not a fighter, *querida*.'

'Yes, I'm sure Sarah would agree.'

'You're jealous.'

The accusation brought an angry flush to her cheeks. It was a nasty taunt made totally unforgivable because it was true.

'Not of Sarah!' She saw the flicker of puzzlement in his eyes and rushed on before he could ask for an explanation. 'Could you be more smug and self-satisfied if you tried? Or is this you trying? I'm not going to cry, if that's what you want.'

Luiz stiffened, a look of frigid affront spreading across his face as he inhaled through flared nostrils. 'You really think I am that sick and sadistic.'

She suddenly saw that the best way to get him to leave was to offend him, hit him directly on his male pride. God knew nothing else was working and there was only so long she could maintain her shaky pose of indifference before her real feelings came tumbling out.

'The fact is what happened was a mistake and I wish I could just have a shower and wash you off my skin and forget about you…'

The expression on his face made her voice fade but she took a deep breath, fixed her eyes on a point over his left shoulder and plunged on, finishing in a rapid, slightly defensive tone.

'I wish I could, but because of the baby I can't. Obviously you can have access to the baby, but I'm not about to make a stupid mistake worse by marrying you.'

'You think us sleeping together was a mistake.'

His outrage struck her as slightly hypocritical.

'Well, if it wasn't a mistake, Luiz, what was it? In my book there is only one reason to get married and that is love.' Short of begging him to say it she couldn't make her request any more obvious and from the flicker in his eyes she knew that he was aware of what she wanted to hear.

Overcome with mortification, she walked over to the door and held it open for him. *Please do not go through, do not leave, love me…*

'I think you should leave.'

He picked up his jacket and coat, slung them over his shoulder.

At the door he turned his head. 'You are being totally irrational.'

She shrugged. 'It's not negotiable. As far as I'm concerned the only reason to get married is love, not duty or financial security.'

He dashed a hand across his face, the gesture intensely weary. 'We will speak when you are being more realistic.'

'I don't want your kind of realism, Luiz.' *I want love— your love.* 'You married for love once—why shouldn't I have the same thing?'

In the act of shrugging on his damp jacket he stopped. 'I will not speak of Rosa with you.'

'What makes you think I want to?' she exclaimed as her feelings burst through her barrier of outward indifference with a rush. 'Your perfect paradise marriage…who could compete? Polish your memories and take them to bed with you. I hope they keep you warm, because I won't! What makes you think any woman wants the man she is in bed with, the man she has just given…' Her voice broke and she took a step back, fending off the hand he extended to her with an angry shake of her head. 'I really don't want to marry a man who reaches for me in the night and calls me by his dead wife's name.'

A look of stark shock froze on Luiz's face. 'I did that?'

'You did.'

'That's why you left without a word?'

'I don't much warm to the idea of a man making love to me while he's thinking of someone else. You would grow to resent this baby.' She pressed a hand to her stomach and ignored his harsh protest. 'Because he'll never be Rosa's baby any more than I'll ever be Rosa.'

'That would never happen, Nell. It *has* never happened. When I am with you I can think of nothing else but you. When I am not with you,' he added with a hard laugh, 'the world seems empty. You are under my skin, in my blood—you are so enmeshed with me nothing short of surgery could remove you. And the baby I will love for himself.'

Nell turned her head, refusing to recognise the urgent note of harsh, anguished sincerity in his voice—she couldn't. 'You have issues, Luiz—face it and them, then we might have something to discuss.'

She opened the door and he walked through.

Luiz walked down the path listening to the sounds of her wild sobbing inside. They cut like a knife.

CHAPTER FIFTEEN

IN A previous reincarnation the small-town library had been a chapel and the acoustics were still excellent. A pencil dropped on the mezzanine level that housed the computer terminals could be heard at the librarian's desk tucked away at the back of the ground-floor library proper.

Nell, who was sitting in an alcove beneath the balcony, a book on her knee, wide-eyed toddlers sitting around her on cushions, heard the sound of footsteps as someone walked up the aisle between the high shelves, but she didn't turn around as she closed the book. She did, however, tilt her head towards a group of teenage girls who were hanging over the balcony, their shrill girlish giggles drawing a few glances from people below. Some were less tolerant than others.

She caught their eyes and shook her head, miming a zipping motion across her lips. They lowered the levels of their giggles while one mimed back a swooning action and stabbed her finger towards a figure walking up the aisle between the rows of tall shelves.

Nell closed the book on her lap with an air of finality and explained to the toddlers with genuine regret—the innocence and enthusiasm of the pre-schoolers always made story time a favourite part of Nell's day—that they could have another story on Friday but right now she had a lot of work to do.

She frowned a little as the teenagers' volume rose again and turned her head, idly curious to see what young man had got the group so animated.

The world swam slightly out of focus and she forgot how to breathe as she put an identity to the tall figure who was approaching the spot where she sat, her face bathed in the gold light that filtered through the arched ecclesiastical window behind her.

For several seconds her brain froze. It refused to accept the information it was being given.

He couldn't be here, not here, not now…not ever. This was her safe workaday world. The only place this could happen, and it did, several times a day, was in the privacy of Nell's own wilful imagination. Had things gone one step further in the week since she'd given him his marching orders? Was she hallucinating…?

A quick furtive glance around the place revealed that if she was so was every other female under ninety in the place!

They were all staring.

Nell's relief was short-lived. Luiz was here and she had lost the ability to move, she was chained to the ground with a combination of sheer longing and lust.

The emotions crowded in on her. She had told herself the next time this happened she would be in control. If she had been capable Nell would have laughed—*control*? What a joke!

Her eyes ate him up hungrily… God, but she had missed him, how much she hadn't allowed herself to acknowledge until now. She blinked, hard unshed tears blurring her vision. Damn him, no wonder all eyes were on him, no wonder her heart was being squeezed in a vice—he was beautiful, the epitome of masculinity.

In a sack he would make heads turn, but dressed like this in a dark designer suit that emphasised his lean, athletic, Greek-god frame he had a face that surpassed Olympian or Hollywood heartthrob standards.

As she watched him a wave of despondency swept over Nell. The fact they lived in different worlds had never been more apparent.

Here in her world the qualities that made Luiz stand out in the most glamorous and exotic locations were even more marked. Even from fifty feet away you could feel the self-assurance, authority, and electric sex appeal he projected like an invisible aura.

As he drew closer Nell could see other things, like the tension that drew the golden skin taut across the incredible bones of his face and the gleam of steely determination that glowed in his eyes that gave him an air of gorgeous menace—he was a man on a mission.

The question was what mission?

She gave her head a little shake and said in a hard little voice, 'Get real, Nell!' You were in big trouble when you allowed your fantasies to intrude into real life. If he was a man in love he was hiding it well—unless love made him as mad as hell!

Luiz thrust his hand in his pocket and pulled out the contents of the parcel that had landed on his desk that morning. His jaw hardened as his fingers closed around it—the symbolism had been obvious, but if she thought she could excise him from her life he was here to make her realise that was not going to happen.

Nell barely noticed as the book fell from her nerveless fingers and onto the floor, or registered the mothers who had begun to collect their offspring, most finding a reason to linger as the tall, utterly gorgeous, rampantly male figure drew closer.

Struggling to cope with her fluttering heart, she was oblivious to the collective fluttering of every female within a fifty-yard radius. By the time Luiz finally stopped a few feet away and stood there, one hand dug in the pocket of his dark jacket, the other sweeping his lush hair, which since their last meeting had grown, away from his forehead, Nell felt physically sick.

Brace yourself, Nell, she told herself. Don't lose it, girl. She picked up the book she had dropped on the floor and adopted an exaggerated expression of surprise as she straightened up.

'Luiz? Sorry, I didn't see you there.' Nell struggled not to wince. Luiz might be extraordinarily lacking in vanity considering he was a lot of people's idea of perfect—or was that just hers?—but even he was not going to swallow that.

'Some things do not change.'

But he had, Luiz reflected, and there was no going back to the man he had been. He didn't intend to do so; his life for the first time in years was going forward. A flicker of tenderness warmed the somber, shadowy darkness of his eyes as he added huskily, 'You still lie very badly, *querida*.'

'You shouldn't be here,' she husked. 'We had an agreement...' Her eyes drank him in, her nostrils widening as her starved senses inhaled the scent of his body. She took a step back and almost tripped over one of the bright floor cushions.

In her head she could see his arms opening and her walking into them. She blinked to clear the scarily real product of her wishful thinking.

'Hello, Nell, and for the record I agreed to nothing.'

'What are you doing here?' She missed the casual she was aiming for by about a million miles and produced shaky scared.

The muscles in his brown throat worked convulsively as the knot of emotion behind his breastbone hardened. 'I came to see you.'

'You did?'

'You look...' He stopped, unable to continue as the impulse to gather her in his arms became overwhelming.

Why was he fighting it? It was where she belonged.

Nell, practically able to feel the tension that rolled off his rigid body in waves, inserted, 'Well, I can't look much worse than you do. When was the last time you had a decent meal?'

'Meal?' he echoed, looking at her as though she had gone mad. 'I've no time for food.'

Nell hid her anxiety behind a sarcastic façade. 'You make it sound optional.'

'I have not come here to discuss dietary requirements.'

'You should not be here at all. I'm at work.' She swallowed as tears filled her eyes. 'Please, Luiz, I really can't take this. You…don't, Jack,' she added, directing a distracted glance towards the small figure with a grubby face and very sticky hands who pulled urgently at Luiz's immaculately tailored trouser leg.

She privately blessed the child for the interruption. Another second and she might have said something embarrassingly stupid. 'I'm sorry, your suit…'

'Relax…' Luiz recommended. Dropping down into a graceful squat, head tilted a little to one side, he looked at the chubby-faced child. 'It's fine.'

Watching him smile at the toddler made Nell's heart squeeze in her chest. Her hands went to her stomach. He would make a great dad. Was she being totally selfish refusing to marry him? Did she have the right to deprive her baby of a full-time dad?

She shook her head. A week earlier it had all seemed perfectly straightforward, but the intervening time had lessened her conviction—was she doing the right thing? What were the right reasons for marriage? Was compromise so bad?

Feeling torn apart by the arguments going round and round in her head, Nell wrapped her arms around herself and hugged tight in a protective gesture. It was impossible to make an objective decision when she ached so much to be with him it physically hurt.

Luiz, a smile curving his lips, glanced up at her. Nell,

unable to hide her feelings—it was so damn exhausting and he was so damn gorgeous—watched his expression change, the humour fade, and saw the flicker of male satisfaction replace it in his dark eyes.

A second firm tug on his trouser leg dragged Luiz's attention back to the child.

'What can I do for you, Jack?'

The little boy fixed him with a critical eye. 'You're big, but not as big as my dad,' he added loyally.

'I expect you will be big one day like your dad.'

'Have you got a dog?'

'I do have a dog.'

'He's got a dog!' Jack shouted to anyone who would listen. 'I want a dog.' He thought about it a bit and added, 'I *need* a dog. My mum says dogs are—'

Nell took him by the shoulders and gently but firmly turned him around. 'Say goodbye, Jack, your mum is here.'

Jack spotted his mother and trotted off.

'Nice kid.'

Nell nodded. 'It's a lovely age. Jack,' she explained with a strained laugh, 'has something of a one-track mind.'

She watched through her lashes as Luiz rose to his feet with effortless elegance.

'I find myself in a similar position.' Despite being spoken in a soft voice, the emotion-packed statement emerged with a force that rocked Nell like an emotional force ten.

She swallowed, noticing again the signs of stress and tension in his face. Always lean, he appeared to have dropped several pounds that added a few more hollows and planes to his chiselled features.

He dug into his pocket and produced a small velvet box. Nell knew what was in it before he opened it.

Luiz watched, the strength of his frowning displeasure cranked up several notches as she tucked her hands behind her back. Did she think he was going to force it back onto her finger?

Actually, now that he thought about it, the idea had merit!

'So you got it, then,' she said brightly as the multi-faceted stone caught the light.

'I got it,' he confirmed grimly.

Nell glanced up, registered the barely suppressed anger in his face and looked away. 'Is there a problem?'

The ring had seemed fine when she had finally managed to get it off, it was her finger that had been bruised and swollen. She absently rubbed the bare finger; it had healed, the bruises were barely noticeable but the bruises inside would, she feared, never go away.

Well, they won't while you've got an attitude like that, girl. Stop whining; stop mooning around after him. He doesn't love you and he never will so suck it up and get on with it. This baby doesn't need a tragic loser as a mum. She took a deep breath and lifted her chin, but couldn't help flinching as he yelled.

'Yes, there's a problem!' he gritted through clenched teeth, his fury fuelled by the fact she had actually recoiled from him. Did she think he would hurt her? *Madre de Dios,* he would have walked across hot coals to protect her from pain.

'I thought you might just have been passing and thought, Gosh, yes, why don't I drop in on Nell, embarrass her in front of her colleagues and abuse her a bit? Well, if that was your intention, Luiz—full marks!'

'I am not trying to hurt you, Nell! Why do you think I'm here?' he added, struggling to shed some of his anger. Not terribly rational anger when you recognized, as he reluctantly did, that, rather than walking across hot coals—noble but not overly practical—it might have been better if he hadn't hurt her in the first place.

'Think?' Thinking required a brain that functioned and could say something other than, Love me—love me!

Conscious her laugh was making him look at her strangely, she gave her head a little shake. Focus, focus…what was the question? Why? Clearly not to ask her to rethink the marriage proposal—which was good, she told herself, because nothing had changed.

'I don't have the faintest!' she admitted after a silence. 'But while you're here do you mind lowering your voice? This is a library, not a football stadium!'

'Why did you send the ring back?' he said, totally ignoring her request.

She shook her head. For a man with a mind like a steel trap the question did not strike her as taxing. 'You came all this way to ask me that? What was wrong with a phone?'

He arched a sardonic brow. 'You would not have answered it.'

Nell's eyes slid self-consciously from his. 'Well under the circumstances I could hardly keep it.'

'You can keep my child.' His eyes slid to her still-flat stomach as he spoke.

Nell's eyes flew to his face.

'But you cannot keep my ring?'

'Will you lower your voice?' she hissed, glancing over her shoulder at people who were pretending they weren't listening to every word he was saying. 'I like this job and I don't want to lose it!' Taking a step closer and lowering her voice, Nell added, 'And it isn't just your child.'

Luiz, who made no attempt to lower his voice, accused loudly, 'It is not me who has forgotten this child has two parents.'

'I haven't forgotten anything, Luiz.' Her chin sank to her chest as she admitted in a broken whisper, 'I wish I could.'

How was she meant to live a normal life when her every waking moment was haunted by memories of the short time they had spent together?

Luiz hooked a finger under her chin and forced her face

up to his. 'You're crying?' His immunity to female tears was totally lacking as she shook her head in denial.

Luiz looked around, frustration stamped on his dark features. 'Is there somewhere private we can be?' He turned his autocratic glare on the efficient-looking woman who was approaching them with purpose. She withstood the contact for a few seconds before she suddenly discovered she was needed elsewhere.

Nell, watching the 'cross to the other side of the road' moment, thought, So this is what it feels like to be on a sinking ship. Though she couldn't really blame Lydia; it would take a very brave person or, in her case, a total fool to take on Luiz Santoro.

'Thanks, Luiz,' she said thickly. 'That was my boss. I've probably lost my job.'

'Do not be foolish.'

Good advice, Nell admitted, her eyes drifting with helpless longing over his lean face, but way too late.

'Well?'

She looked at him blankly and shook her head.

'Somewhere private?' he reminded her.

Nell struggling for control, nodded mutely and pointed in the direction of a door to their left.

Luiz followed the direction of her shaking finger and nodded and, sliding a hand along her shoulders, said, 'Come.'

It was not a suggestion and Nell, for once not disputing his autocratic decree and overpoweringly conscious of the eyes that followed their progress, allowed herself to be directed towards the staff room.

To Nell's relief it was empty. She reached out and grabbed the shelf above the radiator to steady herself. 'Do you ever make a request or do you always issue orders?'

Luiz, who was looking around the small room with an expression of distaste, looked genuinely bewildered by the husky accusation, which he chose not to respond to. Instead he gave his damning verdict on their private place. 'This is a cupboard.'

'A cupboard in your world is a staff room in mine. But what has happened to my manners? Have a seat.' She made a grand sweeping gesture towards one of the two chairs in the room. 'Or a cup of tea?' She gestured towards the kettle and two mugs that stood beside a small sink. The room boasted a small coffee table too.

Luiz ignored the frivolous invitations and carried on standing there, his eyes trained with unnerving intensity on her face, looking big, outrageously sexy and totally out of place in the basic room.

It might not be the cupboard he claimed, but it felt like it with him in it. Her hand went to her throat. She knew the walls of the room were not closing in on her but the illusion was very real.

At his sides Luiz's hands clenched into white-knuckled fists; he could not bear being responsible for her misery. 'You are still crying,' he accused, a nerve clenching in his lean cheek as he watched a tear silently slide down her cheek.

'What if I am?' Nell sniffed with husky belligerence. 'Why wouldn't I be crying? I can't forget a single second we had together, not one second—you're stuck in my head for ever.' She lifted a shaking hand and struck her forehead a glancing blow with the heel of her hand before pressing it palm flat to her chest. 'You're stuck in my—' She stopped abruptly and groaned, 'Oh, God!'

Tears pouring in earnest down her cheeks, she tried to turn away, but was prevented by the big hands that fell heavily to her shoulders. 'Let me go, Luiz!' she begged, aiming a feeble blow at his iron-hard chest, but somehow she ended up laying her head there and sighing as his long fingers moved gently over her hair. 'I can't do…'

'*Never!*'

Nell's face slowly turned up to his. Caution and hope

competed in her eyes as she looked up at him. 'N-never?' she repeated slowly.

'I cannot let you go, *mi querida*.'

'Because of the baby?'

'Leave the baby out of this.'

Nell gave a bitter laugh. Her feelings were ambiguous when he didn't prevent her pulling away from him. 'Easy for you to say—you're not throwing up every morning.'

'Has it been very bad for you?'

When she read the concern and self-reproach in his face Nell felt instantly remorseful. 'I'm fine, I'm not trying to make you feel guilty... It's just not something I can forget about, and how can it not be part of this conversation when if it wasn't for the baby you wouldn't even be here?' she observed sadly.

'You never asked me.'

It was his odd strained manner as much as the abrupt change of subject that made her blink at him in confusion. 'Never asked you what?'

'What track my single-track mind runs along.'

'One track,' she corrected absently. The flammable quality in his unblinking stare was making it hard for her to cling to the shreds of her composure—breathing she had given up on entirely. She wasn't sure if it was lack of oxygen or the mixture of anticipation and apprehension tying her stomach in knots that was responsible for the buzzing in her ears.

'I have a *one*-track mind.' His sensual lips twitched at the correction, but his manner remained just as intense as he continued to speak, '*One*-track when it comes to one beautiful witch with eyes that see into my soul.'

'Me?' she said in a small voice.

'You, *querida*.'

He smiled and the rush of emotion that surged through Nell made her knees sag in ecstatic relief. 'You think about me?'

Luiz bent his head and brushed her delicate eyelids with his lips before framing her face in his hands and declaring in a voice that shook with emotion, 'I go to sleep thinking about you, I wake up thinking about you and in between I think about you, Nell…' He dragged a not quite steady hand through his dark hair and admitted, 'This situation needs to be dealt with—I am not functioning well.' As understatements went this was massive.

Despite the incredible nature of his confession and the way her optimistic romantic heart had gone into happy-ending mode, Nell regarded him with wary caution.

'How do you propose dealing with it?'

'Marry me.'

She turned her head away to hide the tears that sprang to her eyes. 'We have been here before, Luiz.'

'I know, and I know why you said no. It was not because you don't love me, because I think…no, I *know* you do, Nell. You don't have to say anything…'

Nell looked him and thought, Good, because at that moment she couldn't have spoken if her life depended on it.

'Marry me, Nell, because I love you. Is that not what you wanted me to say, *mi querida?*'

Nell shook her head, unable to allow herself to believe the message that shone in his incredible eyes. 'You're saying this now because you know that's what you think I want to hear…?' She couldn't bear for him to say the things she longed to hear if he didn't mean them—it would be too painful. 'I can't bear it!'

Luiz felt the broken whisper like a knife to his heart. He stepped into her, his hands closing over the feminine curve of her hips, moulding her soft body into his hard angularity as he drew her towards him until they stood thigh to thigh. He breathed in her scent… *Madre de Dios*, he had missed her.

'No, I'm saying it now because I can't keep it in any longer.'

Nell heard with wonder the total sincerity in his voice and saw infinite tenderness in his face as he looked at her. She felt her doubts and uncertainties vaporize; she felt lighter than she had done in weeks.

'No, I'm saying it now,' he continued in the same driven voice, 'because I want the world to hear.'

Nell loosed one hand and, with a strangled sob that caused his brow to crease in anxiety, she dashed it across her tear-filled eyes.

He cupped the side of her face with one big hand and rubbed his thumb across the gentle curve of her cheek.

'Don't cry,' he begged. 'I cannot bear it. I have missed you so much, *mi querida*. I have been a fool, a coward.' The self-disgust in his face spoke volumes. 'I told myself that a man only loves once in his life, because it seemed to me that a man could only survive losing the sort of love I had with Rosa once. After she died I retreated into myself and constructed walls.

'But I realise now that I didn't really survive. Part of me has been dead, Nell.' He looked at her with glowing, loving eyes and clasped her hand to his chest, pressing it against his heart. 'Until you, *mi querida,* woke it up.'

A little cry was wrenched from Nell's aching throat. The tears that clung to her eyelashes were cleansing.

There was wonder in his eyes as his glance drifted across her face. 'You are incredible, so beautiful—no wonder I fell in love with you at first sight.'

Nell's throat ached with emotion as she lifted her hand to his lips and said, 'Hush, you don't have to say that—'

She cut him off with a shake of her head as she struggled to be grown up and mature about this. He had baggage—it was not rational to expect him to come to her as a blank slate.

Rosa had been his first love. She could ask him to choose between them and he might even feel he should, but Nell knew that in the long run he would resent her for it.

'I believe you love me, but I know that you'll never love me the way you loved Rosa.' She didn't want him to feel he had to compensate by pretending he felt things he didn't.

'I loved Rosa not as I love you?' He tilted his head to one side as if considering her words. Then nodded and said, 'This is true.'

Nell smiled in the face of her misery and told herself she could settle for being his last love and not his first.

'That has been my problem. What I felt for Rosa was slow, deep and gentle. What I felt for you, on the other hand…' He sucked in a deep shuddering breath that lifted his chest as, with an expression of wonder, he trailed his fingers over the curve of her cheek. 'What I felt for you was passionate, extreme and intense. It was drawn,' he said, pressing a clenched fist to his chest, 'from somewhere deep inside me. I told myself it was lust, a violent chemical reaction that had no staying power, because I felt guilty.'

'Guilty?' she echoed, startled. The possibility had never crossed her mind.

He inclined his dark head. 'Yes, guilty. Rosa had known me inside out and I her, yet you, a stranger, you challenged me on every level, and at the same time made me feel things I had never felt before…and your face…your lovely face, without trying, you, your face…' Abstracted, wondering warmth entered his eyes as he stared down at her and then, as if unable to resist the temptation, pressed a hard, hungry kiss to her soft lips.

Nell melted, then as he lifted his head, her glowing eyes focused on his beloved face, she no longer tried to repress the words she had ached to give voice to. 'I love you, Luiz.'

The breath left Luiz's lungs on one deep relieved gasp. A slow smile spread across his face, wiping away the lines of strain around his mouth and removing the last shadows from his eyes. 'You have no idea how much I needed to hear you say that.'

The husky confession moved Nell profoundly. It had not occurred to her until that moment that Luiz, with his supremely confident manner, might nurture any doubts. 'I thought you *knew* I loved you,' she teased with husky warmth.

His shoulders lifted in a shrug. 'I couldn't let myself think anything else or I would have gone mad. You see how much power you have over me.'

Nell, her eyes shining like stars, laid her hand lightly against the side of his face. He turned his head and pressed an open-mouthed kiss to her palm.

'I promise I won't misuse it.'

'If you do I will probably deserve it. When I think of all the pain that could have been avoided if I hadn't been such a blind, stubborn fool!' With a self-contemptuous grimace he shook his head in disbelief. 'I love you, but I fought it with every cell of my body. I wouldn't allow myself...can you forgive me? Can you understand it felt like the ultimate betrayal to her memory?'

Nell, who knew she could forgive him anything except not loving her, did not respond to his anguished question. She fully appreciated how difficult this was for Luiz, a man who kept his own counsel, who did not share his feelings easily, to reveal so much of himself this way and she did not want to interrupt the flow of startling confidences that fell from his lips.

'Since Rosa died I had never invested emotionally in a relationship. I never wanted to, then you came, and if I had admitted even to myself that I loved you...?' He shook his head. 'I was in denial, and then you called me on it—you accused me of romanticising my marriage. I was so angry that I—'

Nell's eyes shone with regret as she caught his hand. 'I'm sorry, Luiz. I shouldn't have said what I did. It was—'

'It was the truth, *querida*,' he cut in.

Shock washed across Nell's face. 'But you loved Rosa—you had a perfect marriage...?'

He released a sardonic crack of laughter. 'Perfect as in paradise?'

The reminder of her harsh words brought a regretful flush to Nell's cheeks.

'The fact is we had problems.'

Nell's eyes widened. 'You did…?'

He nodded and looked amused by her amazement. 'My memory has been very selective. I chose not to remember them. Who knows—if she had not died our marriage might have been good, it might indeed have been *perfect,* we might have grown together, but it is equally possible that we might have grown apart. The signs were there.'

The forthright admission shocked and, if she was honest, reassured Nell, who felt relieved to have the pressure to conform to some saintly standard of perfect wife removed.

'Rosa was a free spirit and my success financially was something she thought staid and boringly conventional. And in my turn I was not overly enamoured by her crystals, alternative therapies and arty friends in kaftans. We were both very young and not very tolerant. She was ready for a family and I was not.

'I think,' he admitted, 'I was doing Rosa a disservice by remembering her as some insipid saint. She was more than that. But Rosa is the past, a memory.' His voice thickened as his finger straightened over hers. 'You, *mi querida,* are the future. My future.'

Love shone in Nell's luminous eyes as she raised the hand she held to her face and curved the long brown fingers around her cheek. 'Our future, Luiz, together,' she corrected, a smile like the sun breaking out on her face as she added huskily, 'I like the way that sounds.'

With a laugh he gathered her to him, raining kisses on her upturned features. 'I too like it. I feel as if I have been alone for such a long time, and now I have a family.' He laid a hand on her stomach and smiled. 'I will be afraid to close my eyes tonight in case I wake up and discover this was all a marvellous dream.'

Nell drew herself up on tiptoe and took his beloved face between her hands. 'Oh, that won't be a problem. I hadn't actually planned on you getting much sleep tonight.'

Luiz, his spine tingling at her wicked little laugh, could find no fault with her plan. 'We could start not sleeping right now.'

'In case you forgot, Luiz, I'm at work.'

'When I look at you, *mi querida,* I forget everything but my love for you.'

Enchanted by the declaration, Nell took him by the hand. 'I think that under the circumstances they might let me leave early today... Luiz...have you ever seen that film where Richard Gere—?'

Before she had finished he had scooped her into his arms. As he kicked open the door he looked down at her with love that took her breath away glowing in his marvellous eyes. 'Our future, *querida,* starts now.'

Nell gave a contented sigh. Her future suddenly looked as though it might be very interesting indeed.

* * * * *

Kay Young returned to woozy consciousness to find that she was lying on a soft sofa beneath a heap of quilts near a cheerfully burning fire. When she tried to move, however, everything hurt, and she groaned.

At once she heard a sound, then a stranger with a hard, harsh face was squatting beside her. "Shh," he said softly. "You're safe here. I promise."

"I have to go," she said weakly, struggling against pain. "He'll find me. He can't find me."

"Easy, lady," he said quietly. "You're hurt. No one's going to find you here."

"He will," she said desperately, terror clutching at her insides. "He always finds me!"

"Easy," he said again. "There's a blizzard outside. No one's getting here tonight, not even the doctor. I know, because I tried."

"Doctor? I don't need a doctor! I've got to get away."

"There's nowhere to go tonight," he said levelly. "And if I thought you could stand, I'd take you to a window and show you."

But even as she tried once more to pull away the quilts, she remembered something else: this man had been gentle when he'd found her beside the road, even when she had kicked and clawed. He hadn't hurt her.

Terror receded just a bit. She looked at him and detected signs of true concern there.

The terror eased another notch and she let her head sag on the pillow. "He always finds me," she whispered.

"Not here. Not tonight. That much I can guarantee."

Will Kay's mysterious rescuer protect her
from her worst fears?
Find out in HER HERO IN HIDING
by New York Times *bestselling author Rachel Lee.*
Available June 2010,
only from Silhouette® Romantic Suspense.

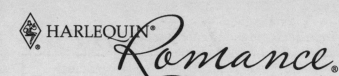

HARLEQUIN® *Romance*®

GIRLS' *Weekend in* VEGAS

Four friends, four dream weddings!

On a girly weekend in Las Vegas, best friends Alex, Molly, Serena and Jayne are supposed to just have fun and forget men, but they end up meeting their perfect matches! Will the love they find in Vegas stay in Vegas?

Find out in this sassy, fun and wildly romantic miniseries all about love and friendship!

Saving Cinderella! by MYRNA MACKENZIE
Available June

Vegas Pregnancy Surprise by SHIRLEY JUMP
Available July

Inconveniently Wed! by JACKIE BRAUN
Available August

Wedding Date with the Best Man
by MELISSA MCCLONE
Available September

www.eHarlequin.com

HR17663

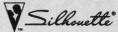

LARGER-PRINT BOOKS!

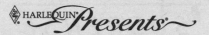 HARLEQUIN *Presents*

PASSION GUARANTEED SEDUCTION

GET 2 FREE LARGER-PRINT NOVELS PLUS 2 FREE GIFTS!

YES! Please send me 2 FREE LARGER-PRINT Harlequin Presents® novels and my 2 FREE gifts (gifts are worth about $10). After receiving them, if I don't wish to receive any more books, I can return the shipping statement marked "cancel". If I don't cancel, I will receive 6 brand-new novels every month and be billed just $4.55 per book in the U.S. or $5.24 per book in Canada. That's a saving of at least 13% off the cover price! It's quite a bargain! Shipping and handling is just 50¢ per book.* I understand that accepting the 2 free books and gifts places me under no obligation to buy anything. I can always return a shipment and cancel at any time. Even if I never buy another book, the two free books and gifts are mine to keep forever.

176/376 HDN E5NG

Name	(PLEASE PRINT)	
Address		Apt. #
City	State/Prov.	Zip/Postal Code

Signature (if under 18, a parent or guardian must sign)

Mail to the **Harlequin Reader Service:**
IN U.S.A.: P.O. Box 1867, Buffalo, NY 14240-1867
IN CANADA: P.O. Box 609, Fort Erie, Ontario L2A 5X3

Not valid for current subscribers to Harlequin Presents Larger-Print books.

**Are you a subscriber to Harlequin Presents books
and want to receive the larger-print edition?
Call 1-800-873-8635 today!**

* Terms and prices subject to change without notice. Prices do not include applicable taxes. Sales tax applicable in N.Y. Canadian residents will be charged applicable provincial taxes and GST. Offer not valid in Quebec. This offer is limited to one order per household. All orders subject to approval. Credit or debit balances in a customer's account(s) may be offset by any other outstanding balance owed by or to the customer. Please allow 4 to 6 weeks for delivery. Offer available while quantities last.

Your Privacy: Harlequin Books is committed to protecting your privacy. Our Privacy Policy is available online at www.eHarlequin.com or upon request from the Reader Service. From time to time we make our lists of customers available to reputable third parties who may have a product or service of interest to you. If you would prefer we not share your name and address, please check here. ☐

Help us get it right—We strive for accurate, respectful and relevant communications. To clarify or modify your communication preferences, visit us at www.ReaderService.com/consumerchoice.

HPLP10R

Love Inspired

Bestselling author

JILLIAN HART

brings you another heartwarming story
from

the

GRANGER FAMILY RANCH

Rancher Justin Granger hasn't seen his high school sweetheart
since she rode out of town with his heart. Now she's back, with
sadness in her eyes, seeking a job as his cook and housekeeper.
He agrees but is determined to avoid her…until he discovers
that her big dream has always been him!

The Rancher's Promise

*Available June
wherever books are sold.*

Coming Next Month

in **Harlequin Presents® EXTRA.** Available May 11, 2010.

#101 THE COSTANZO BABY SECRET
Catherine Spencer
Claiming His Love-Child

#102 HER SECRET, HIS LOVE-CHILD
Tina Duncan
Claiming His Love-Child

#103 HOT BOSS, BOARDROOM MISTRESS
Natalie Anderson
Strictly Business

#104 GOOD GIRL OR GOLD-DIGGER?
Kate Hardy
Strictly Business

Coming Next Month

in **Harlequin Presents®.** Available May 25, 2010:

#2921 A NIGHT, A SECRET...A CHILD
Miranda Lee

#2922 FORBIDDEN: THE SHEIKH'S VIRGIN
Trish Morey
Dark-Hearted Desert Men

#2923 THE MASTER'S MISTRESS
Carole Mortimer

#2924 GREEK TYCOON, WAYWARD WIFE
Sabrina Philips
Self-Made Millionaires

#2925 THE PRINCE'S ROYAL CONCUBINE
Lynn Raye Harris

#2926 INNOCENT IN THE ITALIAN'S POSSESSION
Janette Kenny

HPCNMBPA0510

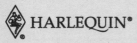

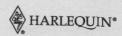

HARLEQUIN®

Showcase

On sale May 11, 2010

Reader favorites from the most talented voices in romance

Save $1.00 on the purchase of 1 or more Harlequin® Showcase books.

SAVE
$1.00 on the purchase of 1 or more Harlequin® Showcase books.

Coupon expires Oct 31, 2010. Redeemable at participating retail outlets.
Limit one coupon per purchase. Valid in the U.S.A. and Canada only.

52609015

Canadian Retailers: Harlequin Enterprises Limited will pay the face value of this coupon plus 10.25¢ if submitted by customer for this product only. Any other use constitutes fraud. Coupon is nonassignable. Void if taxed, prohibited or restricted by law. Consumer must pay any government taxes. Void if copied. Nielsen Clearing House ("NCH") customers submit coupons and proof of sales to Harlequin Enterprises Limited, P.O. Box 3000, Saint John, NB E2L 4L3, Canada. Non-NCH retailer—for reimbursement submit coupons and proof of sales directly to Harlequin Enterprises Limited, Retail Marketing Department, 225 Duncan Mill Rd., Don Mills, ON M3B 3K9, Canada.

5 65373 00076 2   (8100)0 11651

U.S. Retailers: Harlequin Enterprises Limited will pay the face value of this coupon plus 8¢ if submitted by customer for this product only. Any other use constitutes fraud. Coupon is nonassignable. Void if taxed, prohibited or restricted by law. Consumer must pay any government taxes. Void if copied. For reimbursement submit coupons and proof of sales directly to Harlequin Enterprises Limited, P.O. Box 880478, El Paso, TX 88588-0478, U.S.A. Cash value 1/100 cents.

® and TM are trademarks owned and used by the trademark owner and/or its licensee.
© 2009 Harlequin Enterprises Limited

HSCCOUP0410